GIVEN

NOT

TAKEN

By Kenneth Thomas Sr.

ISBN 978-0-692-52958-4

Library of Congress Control Number 2015951507

Printed in the United States of America

First Printing: February 2016

CHAPTERONE

~~~~~~

L aying totally relaxed in his bunk, Major Calvin Hollaway re-read the handwritten letter he'd discovered packed within the inner pocket of the canvas rucksack. He held the letter to his nose and breathed in the scent of her peppermint lotion. Even after the third reading and the third long inhale of her scent, his heart raced with anticipation, and he read the note again as if for the first time.

Baby, I just want you to know, I am so happy you're in my life. You are the man I call my husband, my friend, my soulmate. And. I really need you to know this.

He nodded and smiled as the words travelled through his brain. "I've known it since I was four," he said, nearly whispering. For a quick moment, he saw the image of his four-year-old self admiring her—a small, brown-eyed, three year old learning to jump rope.
He kept reading.

The worse part of my life was when I had to leave you to do my pediatric residency at John Hopkins. Baby, I can't tell you how happy I was to see you when you arrived at Fort Benning on the day we were sworn in together as proud U.S. Army officers.

His eyes lowered and scanned the green wool blanket. With his left hand, he traced the stenciled letters U and S of the government-issued blanket.

I keep thinking about the last time we were together ummm, you sure do know how to leave a lasting impression on your woman. The way you leave light and love through me is remarkable! When you placed your lips on my belly and then laid your head on it, saying you wish there was a baby inside me, my soul melted. The day that happens I believe you are going to be a wonderful father. I can't wait to see little soldiers running around looking like the perfect blend of us. I can't wait to start popping out Hollaway babies. I want eight. As fast as you can put them in are as fast as I want to birth them.

"Eight?" He said while shaking his head and grinning. A warm breeze wrapped around his shoulders, and he continued reading on to the next page.

Okay, dear sir, Captain Hollaway. I know you don't like all this mushy stuff, so I'll see you when you get to our camp. Oh, by the way, there's a special treat wrapped in your bag. It's sewn as a zipper pocket inside your brown satchel. I can't believe I let Stiles convince me to do it. If the Iraqi sol-

diers capture you, you better chew these damn pictures up and swallow them! If these pictures get on TMZ, Momma's going to kill us both no matter where we are! I can hear her now, "What were ya'll thinking, having my baby and all her glory out there for the world to see?!" Truth be told, I don't care. I had fun taking them for you. I thought about you every second while taking them. Enjoy them like you enjoy me. Good day, Captain, I love you and miss you terribly.

-Déjà

"I love you more, Madam Captain," Major Hollaway whispered. Now that he had privacy, he took the lining out of the satchel and retrieved his wife's gift. Laughing out loud, he eagerly unwrapped the parchment paper that covered the aluminum foil holding the portraits.

"Oh, hell yeah!" He said as he pumped his fist in the air.

Slowly, he flipped through all seven, three-inch pictures. Her body was amazingly beautiful. His eyes enjoyed every photograph while his manhood yearned. He turned down the small desk lamp with one click, laid back, and enjoyed the midnight breeze, the touch of his own hand, and the sight of his beautiful wife who was surely thinking of him, too.

After sliding the pictures back into satchel's secret pocket, he turned off the small lamp near his bunk and fell asleep.

~~~~~~

</div>

Three hours later Sergeant Chang walked into the second largest villa on the royal compound, now converted into the officer's quarters. The light from the moon peeked over the brim of his hat and cast a somber shadow across the grey and tan gravel. The middle aged Asian, Non-Commissioned Officer entered Major Hollaway's sleeping quarters as he'd done countless times before. He stood at the foot of the bed, "Major Hollaway," he tried to whisper but it came out more as a whimper of pain. He cleared his throat and quickly squared his shoulders. "Major! Major Hollaway."

Twenty-four hours before, he was Captain Hollaway. So when he initially heard "major" in his sleep, it didn't register. There was always a little adjustment after a fresh promotion. The major shifted his weight in the small bed as he woke. "The colonel would like to see you immediately, sir."

Major Hollaway final sat up and for a moment, he only gazed straight ahead. He ran the palms of his hands down his face until they fell off, landing on the bed behind him and bracing his body.

"What time is it?"

"Zero-three-thirty."

Major Hollaway turned his body to one side of the bed and placed his bare feet on the marble floor.

The quarters of Camp Doha, Kuwait were much better than the tent barracks of Iraq they had just left. The makeshift flooring of pallets that sometimes moved would not be missed. The sturdy cold marble floor in Kuwait was well received, especially during the early morning nature calls.

"Sergeant Chang, I must have been knocked out."

Falling asleep with the thought of making love to his wife led him to dreaming she had conceived. She was telling him the news when the Sergeant woke him.

Major Hollaway stood quickly sliding on his desert battle dress uniform. He felt a buzz of excitement and joy.

"I can't wait until next week when I get to Saudi. I'm going to walk into my wife's camp, and when she sees these gold leaves on my collar, her reaction is going to be simply priceless! You know she bet me she would get promoted to major before me?"

"Yes, sir," Sergeant Chang quickly answered. He turned his back to the major and walked to open the door. Major Hollaway thought his behavior was a little strange. The two always joked about everything, no matter how dangerous the mission was.

Things got even stranger as they walked to Colonel Edward Gaston's quarters. Normally the other three commanders, along with their drivers, would have already joined them in route. But, no one was near.

At the entrance of the office, Sergeant Chang opened the door. He stopped short, saluted, and quickly exited, closing the door softly behind him.

"Major Hollaway reporting as ordered, sir." Major Hollaway saluted and then the colonel.

A prior service enlisted man, Colonel Gaston had everyone's respect. His father suggested it would be best if he enlisted and after a short stint move on to be commissioned. Early on, Colonel Gaston's position was that to become an excellent warrior and leader, he had to first know what it meant to follow. Equipped with a psychology degree from the University of Auburn and the wisdom from generations of remarkable men, the colonel was well-prepared for army life and for leadership.

"Have a seat, son," Colonel Gaston said. The two sat at attention across from each other. Major Hollaway noticed the old pecan-colored man didn't have on his DBSU jacket which was uncommon for senior officers but he knew the colonel's policy. In certain situations, Colonel Gaston never wanted his rank to intimidate his troops. Apparently, this was one of those situations.

The colonel rubbed the palm of his right hand across his thin mustache and over his full lips as he prepared to speak, "It is my unfortunate duty on this the second day of Operation Desert Shield, to inform you of the passing of your wife Captain Déjà Hollaway."

The second those words left the colonel's lips Major Hollaway's heart froze. His body stiffened and the heave of his chest slowed to a near stop. He couldn't breathe. He couldn't blink his eyes. His body—all of his being—had become paralyzed. The only indication he was alive came moments later as tears streamed down his cheeks and began to soak the front of his uniform.

Locked in the same position, he fought to gather himself and managed to ask, "What happened?"

"Her unit had just completed assembling and stocking the field hospital. They were awaiting the final delivery of Red Cross paraphernalia for the doors, windows, and the roof to identify it as a hospital." Colonel Gaston stood and walked to his desk. After shifting through two drawers he pulled out a small, wooden box. Major Hollaway's eyes didn't move from the colonel's empty chair, and his body stayed erect. The colonel selected a blue handkerchief from the box and walked back toward Major Hollaway. Their eyes met.

"Recon saw the convoy and mistook them for enemy troops." He placed the handkerchief in Hollaway's left hand and, with both hands, he helped the major grip the small fabric until he knew Major Hollaway was holding it. He nodded his head slowly and the colonel continued, "Before Captain Hollaway or her company could be correctly identified, action had been taken, and they fell victim to friendly fire."

Holding the handkerchief in his balled fist, Major Hollaway asked, "Where is she?"

"Her body rests in the southwest hangar. Sergeant Chang is waiting to take you to her."

"Are you sure it's Captain Déjà Hollaway?"

"I am sorry to say. Yes."

A knock on the door interrupted them. "Enter," the colonel said as he rose to stand. Sergeant Chang opened the door and said, "I brought the Humvee out front. Are you ready, sir?" Major Hollaway saluted the colonel and turned to follow Sergeant Chang. The ride to the hangar was silent, but loud enough to tear him apart. Morning seemed to have met them once they arrived at the hangar. Sergeant Chang stopped the Humvee at the far right side of the building and got out to open the major's door. Seconds seemed like hours as Major Hollaway managed to get out of the Humvee and inch his way to the steel dome shaped building.

"Take your time, sir. I am here for you," Sergeant Chang said still standing by the Humvee.

The mortuary affairs officer waited by the door as Major Hollaway labored to walk across the short crosswalk. He saluted the major and led him through a winding hall of white walls and small rooms. They stopped at a large, refrigerated room.

The officer opened a large compartment drawer and looked over to the senior officer whose face was stoned with shock and fear. Déjà's body laid in the drawer's center and was wrapped in a black zipped body bag.

Major Hollaway took one step toward the drawer. From the moment the zipper exposed her forehead he knew it was the one he used to kiss. He took in a deep breath and strained to force back the hot vomit rising in his throat.

He slowly nodded for the viewing to continue.

The officer unzipped the bag further down to chest level then quickly zipped it close. He determined that was all the major could stand to see. "I am sorry for your loss, Major Hollaway. Let's go to my office so we can discuss the plans of bringing her home."

He delicately closed the drawer, placing Déjà's body into the large refrigerated walls.

The two walked into the office. Once inside, he gestured for Major Hollaway to sit. He shuffled papers across his desk until he found a folder. Major Hollaway sat quietly.

"We will be able to get her home by commercial flight in a week."

"Commercial?"

"Um, yes, sir."

"How long will it take on a military flight?"

"Two days," the coroner responded as he walked to a coffee pot filled with steaming water. "We thought you would feel more comfortable on a commercial flight." He poured the water into a green mug filled with three tea bags and a fourth a cup of honey.

"Captain Déjà Hollaway is still a military officer of the United States Army and that's how she would want to be brought home. That's how we are going home." Major Hollaway did an about-face and walked out the door leaving the officer holding the hot mug.

~~~~~~

Two days later, Major Hollaway showed up in his dress blues to escort his wife home. The six-foot-six-inch officer's skin was as dark as a smooth piece of shiny blue steel. His head was completely shaved, along with the beard that he was permitted to wear while in the Gulf region. His sunglasses served a dual purpose: to protect his eyes from the brutal desert sun rays and to hide the swelling.

Major Hollaway stood at attention and saluted as his wife's casket, draped with the American flag, was carried pass him by the color guard. They placed her casket in the back of a converted Humvee. At zero six fifteen, the sun peeked.

Major Hollaway looked over to his right about a mile ahead of the airstrip to see the belly of the aircraft opened. It would be used for the journey home. He could see a second group of color guards already in position to load another fallen soldier. A female private saluted then asked, "Sir, is that your only luggage?" She pointed to his single bag.

He returned the salute and said, "Yes, this is it."

She placed it in the back of the Humvee and walked him to the plane. He entered from the side entrance. He stood waiting for the air crew to secure the casket.

"Make sure the head is placed the same direction the aircraft nose is facing," directed the officer in charge. After doing so, the detail racketed the straps along the side of the base of the army-issued coffin.

With the casket secured on the C-14, Major Hollaway took a seat to the left of the casket, symbolizing her as having more rank. He sat at attention the entire flight across the Atlantic Ocean.

Nine hours later when they arrived at Naval Air Station in Jacksonville, Florida, both his and her families were there.

Major Hollaway stood to his feet and touched the casket just before putting on his Oakley sunglasses. *I am going to make you proud, Baby. I will be there for them. I will be strong and won't cry until it's all clear. I promise.*

The moment he walked in the corridor, he locked his eyes on Déjà's mother, Mrs. Jordan. With each step, he lost control of his bottom lip that he held with his teeth. He opened his arms as wide as he could to allow her in. His bottom lip now quivered at the speed of a humming bird's flying wings. A river of tears gushed from under his shades.

His own mother stood slightly to the side of him holding her mouth and nodding, letting him know he was right to comfort Mrs. Jordan who needed it more. Mr. Jordan joined in and wrapped his arms around them both.

11

He spoke.

"She has been a lot of first in our family. She is our first and only child. She was the first to graduate college. She was the first female to join the military. We've had a member in the military every generation. She always told me, 'Daddy I'm going to be a soldier just like you.' I can remember it like it was yesterday. I told her, 'No, darling, you are going to be better than Daddy. You are going to be an officer. She said, 'Okay, Daddy. I'm going to be an Officer Soldier, Daddy.' She knew this was a dangerous profession. But she said she had to do it. We lost one in the Civil War. We lost one in Korea. We lost two in World War I. We caught a break in World War II. I lost my brother in Vietnam. She did what she needed to do."

They agreed.

Major Hollaway's father spoke. "Son, the funeral home that will be handling everything is here." He signed the papers and Holmes-Glover-Solomon took her body away. Everyone went over to Déjà family home to reflect—and comfort.

~~~~~~

Major Hollaway sat in the back of the black Cadillac limousine in the first car behind the hearse. He watched family, civil friends, and military as they walked into Bethel Baptist Institutional Church. Captain Stiles walked with their medical commander. Colonel Gaston was the next military member to enter. The service was held in the main sanctuary to accommodate the four thousand medical and military visitors who joined her family and friends. Sergeant Chang knocked on the car door before he opened it. "Sir, they are ready for the family now." Major Hollaway took a deep breath as he moved toward the door.

He stepped out of the limousine alone.

Wearing his darkest pair of Oakley sunglasses, he slowly walked to the entrance of the church. No longer shielded from the sounds of sorrow. The air filled with yelping, moaning, humming, and out right crying. They wrapped around him like a vine of thorns. The entire church stood on their feet as the family walked in to view the body for the last time. His sister Cheryl had to be peeled away from the casket by Déjà's brother, Leo.

Major Hollaway walked alone.

The dress blues he wore had never been worn before. Everything he had on was new, even the glistening pair of patent leather shoes. He had decided this ensemble would be a one-and-done. Everything was going to be boxed up after the ceremony.

He removed his black hat with his right hand and placed it underneath his left arm, just before he walked through the church doors.

With each deliberate step towards her casket, he replayed the journey the two had within the same walls of their church home.

Both parents and Pastor Senior always talked about how he cried so much during their Christening ceremonies and Déjà just watched. He also remembered the day he watched Déjà get baptized. Their wedding day flashed in his mind as he reached halfway down the church's large aisle. Looking straight ahead and fixed on his bride, he felt the expectant eyes of all three families during the slow march: his family, her family and their military family. But this walk was the hardest.

When he finally made it to her casket, Major Hollaway stood over his wife. He slowly placed his hat at the base of the casket, reached into his inside jacket pocket and pulled out the gold leaf major insignia. He gently pinned it on the right lapel of her dress blues and kissed her forehead for the last time.

"Here you go, Major Déjà Hollaway. Thank you, Baby, for showing me heaven on earth."

After the eulogy, Major Hollaway led the family procession out of the church. They stopped just outside the doors to watch the color guard carefully load the casket into the hearse.

Before he got into the limousine, he noticed an overflow of law enforcement agents—state troopers, city police, and county sheriffs—on motorcycles and in unmarked and marked cars escorting the caravan to the grave site.

Sergeant Chang parked the limo and came around to open Major Hollaway's door. Painfully, he stepped out of the car and adjusted his hat. "I don't think I can make it, Chang."

"Just a little longer, sir. She's almost at rest."

"Stay close." He murmured quickly through a quivering bottom lip. Then headed to the tent. His tall frame curved by half of a foot as he bent down to walk underneath the funeral home's green tent. He took his seat and watched the pallbearers place the casket gently on the belts in front of him. To distract his urge to cry, Major Hollaway carefully studied the apparatus that would lower the casket into the ground.

A ten-member honor guard team stood in the distance awaiting their cue to render the volley shots. Seven marksmen held their M16s to their cheeks. One of them stood with the brim of his hat pulled down to the point you could not see his eyes. "Ready. Aim. Fire!" He shouted. A thunderous shot leaving a trail of white smoke rushed from the weapon. "Ready. Aim. Fire!" Again, sound and smoke filled the air. The final command was ordered. "Ready. Aim. Fire!"

Never in Major Hollaway's life had a gunshot sounded so final.

The flag bearer detail removed the five-foot flag from the casket. They folded, tugged, and pulled the rectangle flag into a perfect triangle leaving five stars showing. The sergeant-of-arms slowly and deliberately walked over to her command. The commanding officer stood at attention as he received it. In the same and deliberate manner, he walked over to Major Hollaway and handed the flag to him.

Behind the shades, Major Hollaway cringed with anger and grief. He let his tears fall as he listened to the whimpers of her father.

After the playing of taps, everyone headed back to the church for the repast. But, he and Sergeant Chang remained seated until all cars had left. "I can't leave her here, I can't," Major Hollaway confessed. "Tell them to come lower her now, please." His request was granted.

At that moment, Major Hollaway slid from his chair to his knees and wept inconsolably. His father returned into the tent and sat beside him, and Sergeant Chang stood with his head bowed.

Once his cries quieted, the two walked him back to the limousine. One man held him at his waist. The other held his shoulders. He tried his best to stop weeping but he was powerless. The best he was able to manage to do was release rounds of uncontrollable sniffles that jerked his body violently. With his father beside him and Sergeant Chang driving, Major Hollaway rode away from the woman he'd dedicated his life and service to and the only girl he swore he would ever love.

CHAPTER TWO

~~~~~~

"Guten Morgen, Opa." The five-foot-ten-inch, natural curly haired blonde spoke just before planting a soft kiss on the mature man's forehead. Dr. Ava Kärcher wore blue scrubs and adjusted her ponytail before she took her seat at the breakfast table. It was 4 a.m. and the two sat directly across from each other. Opa was dressed in Hugo Boss from head to toe, a 100 percent cotton white shirt, and a blue cotton tie. His jacket hung on the valet in the corner of the kitchen.

If one didn't know better it could be said they were fraternal twins with a sixty-year age gap. They bore the same piercing sapphire eyes, same strong high cheek bones. At ninety years old, Opa still possessed a full head of hair that was for sure the same blonde locks on Ava's. Now his was a neat and tidy grey.

"Guten Morgen, Ava."

"Morning, Mr. Lang. Would you like tea or coffee?"

"Morning, Gertrude. Coffee, please. I need something to pick me up this morning."

"What about you, Ava?"

"I'll have tea, Auntie Gertrude."

Gertrude and Ava's mom, Silka, were best friends at M.I.T. until her untimely demise, along with her husband in a car accident. Gertrude quickly fell in love with the Lang family starting with the first time she, Silka, and Armin would take turns on the drive to Jacksonville every break. Gertrude's initial plans were to help out until they could find adequate help with little Ava. That was more than thirty years ago.

"How long will you be in surgery today?"

"There is only one scheduled for this morning. Don't you worry about a thing, Opa. Nothing is going to stop me from being at your birthday celebration."

Gertrude made room on the table and placed a fresh batch of wheat and rye bread, along with assorted cheeses, thin slices of ham, turkey, and salmon, six soft-boiled eggs, and a pitcher of papaya juice.

"It means the world to me if you're there. You're all I have left."

"I know, Opa. Don't worry; I will be there."

"Okay."

"Opa. I bought a fitness center last week."

"Why? You don't need the income."

"With the right management the profit margin can quadruple by the second quarter, and the business model can be revamped slightly to create a seamless franchise network. Besides, it just made sense for me. I get to keep my workout crew together. And the ex-owner is running it I am handling the fiscal parts."

"When do you sleep? You are spreading yourself thin."

"I am just like you, Opa. I am your granddaughter. I live by your advice: work hard, so you can play harder."

Opa smiled and nodded. His personal assistant came in the kitchen at that moment. "Master Lang, are you ready?"

"Well, I guess you are right, Ava. We are two of a kind. It's off to work for me also."

Both laughed as Opa took his white, cloth napkin from his lap and wiped his mouth to leave with Roger.

Ava quickly went to the living room window. She watched the black, 6.3 AMG four-door sedan drive off. She smiled as she remembered that was her regular routine when she was a little girl.

Opa's strong pride was evident. For him, if the words made in Germany were printed, that meant top quality, and Opa was all in. Ava adopted his point of view. Truth be told, this was the only acceptable position in the Lang household.

Gertrude noticed Schwarz downstairs in the kitchen. She couldn't remember the last time she saw Schwarz after Ava finished medical school. She had given Schwarz to Ava when she turned four years old. A beautiful Black, crochet yarn doll with long black hair and four outfits that Ava always found a reason to change.

Schwarz was credited as the main reason Ava was color-blind when it came to people. Oma and Opa were certainly proud of that fact due to the plight they'd endured.

Sitting at the kitchen table, Gertrude took a trip back down memory lane and began to change Schwarz's clothes.

Ava went to the bathroom in her wing of the home and changed into her black medical clogs. On her way back, she heard the piano being played downstairs.

Uli Kärcher stood a shade over six-feet on a good day if he had in his double inserts. He always orchestrated a well-collaborated ensemble making sure that every strand of his black hair was in place and his temples well-tapered to hide premature graying. This morning his silk, light blue pajama had a matching robe with the initials U.K. embroiled on the right lapel. He was always well-tanned and freshly manicured. Looking the part of a vice president in the family real-estate empire was just as important as making the deals, he always said.

Ava peeked through the cracked door and watched her husband sitting at the Steinway & Sonspiano playing his best rendition of "Prelude in C Major" by Johan Sebastian Bach.

"Damn! These short ass fingers my mother cursed me with! Why couldn't I have my father's long, fluent fingers? I could have been a classical pianist just like him," he complained to himself.

Ava opened the door all the way and entered. "Uli, you are getting better with each passing day. I can't believe you don't hear that."

"Try telling the Jacksonville Symphony Orchestra that. This will be my fourteenth audition." Uli said with little confidence.

"And you'll be ready." Ava kissed him on his lips. She walked across the hall from the piano room to the home office and brought back five thick envelopes. "I have the packets for the Tamina project to share at the board meeting." She handed the yellow envelopes to him. "Okay, I have them numbered. This is the first one. Place them in your briefcase in this order so your presentation stays concise." Uli kept them in order as he placed them in his briefcase.

"If he asks you about funding, go to the third stack. That is where all your financials are. If he asks about the infrastructure, the fourth stack will answer all those questions. The profit margin is in that stack on page fifty-eight. Now, you know Opa is going to ask about the German contractor, you'll find that in stack one. Do you have everything?"

Uli nodded.

"Don't forget Opa's birthday party tonight. It's important."

"I won't forget." Ava walked through the corridor to the garage. She got in her convertible AMG SL6.5, two-door coup and drove away.

CHAPTER THREE

~~~~~~

Major Hollaway stood a few feet pass and to the right of the two-mile finish line. He bent over and held on to the bottom of his grey army-issued shorts as he took in three deep breaths.

"Nine minutes and thirty-four seconds, Major. Best time in the battalion. You still have it, sir," said the fitness Non-Commissioned Officer and hands him a P.T. card.

He took his card and went up to the S4 department to turn in.

"Major Hollaway," said the Executive Officer. "The CO and I were just talking about you."

"Oh, really, what about, sir?" Major Hollaway didn't care for Major Hudson much at all, and he knew it. Major Hudson wore the title of second in command but Major Hollaway out ranked him by three months.

This would change the day he re-ups.

"The old man will tell you himself. He wants to see you in his office," said Major Hudson.

Major Hollaway walked to the commander's office and knocked.

"Come in."

He stopped a foot in front of the desk and saluted. "Major Hollaway reports as requested, sir."

"At ease, Major. Your re-enlistment date is a month away."

"Yes, sir."

"You aren't going to wait until the last day. Are you, major?"

"Oh no, sir." Major Hollaway said confidently. "I am not going to re-enlist."

"What? Your career is going so well, Major. Why wouldn't you?"

"I have lost my will."

"We all have our days, Major. You're a field grade officer. All the hard work has been done. As a matter of fact, I saw your name on the promotable list."

Major Hollaway stopped for a second but kept focused on his decision.

"Let's look at the obvious," said Colonel Philips. "You are young, tall, fit, an African American with two conflicts behind you. If you don't think DA will take all that under consideration when your photo comes on their desk, you are mistaken."

Major Hollaway leaned forward and looked the colonel directly in his eyes as he spoke. "Colonel Philips, I lost my wife. I lost my life. Every day my alarm went off, I smiled. You know why? God granted me another day to wake up as the husband of Déjà Hollaway. That meant a chance to love her, to hold her, to kiss her, to protect her. I can't help but think I could have done something to change this. I pray every day to make it without her. If God were to give me anything in the world, I would ask for her. Or I would ask him to take me and not her. I wouldn't wish this on the enemy. I can't put on this uniform one day after this commitment is satisfied." Major Hollaway stopped momentarily, then said, "Don't get me wrong. I'm not bitter with the United States Army. This was our duty and Déjà and I both knew this could happen."

He abruptly stopped talking, then saluted.

The colonel nodded and returned the salute. Major Hollaway did an about-face and walked out.

After departing the military, Calvin Hollaway took his grandfather's offer to start a new career as a longshoreman. Even though both worlds were miles apart. One world completely dictated while the other was totally voluntary.

"Calvin. Come in, son. How are you?"

"I'm fine, Poppie. I thought I'd take you up on your offer and try this longshoreman thing."

"You know it's hard work."

"Poppie. I'm not afraid work."

One by one, his grandfather called the five department foremen, starting with the cruise terminal, then the container, raw material, military, and automobile. "This is my grandson. I need him to qualify quickly. Look out for him like I look out for you. I need this transition to be smooth."

Nepotism was the rule and not the exception. Who wouldn't take care of the president's grandson?

When his grandfather retired, Calvin still climbed the career ladder, but on his own merit. In a four-year time frame, Calvin became cruise terminal foreman.

CHAPTER FOUR

~~~~~~

Ullrich Kärcher sat behind his desk in the dark office dressed in his favorite German designer, Hugo Boss, from head to toe. He wore a Hugo Boss white, pure cotton shirt, black tie, dark grey slacks, and dark grey socks. Even his well-polished black shoes were from Hugo Boss.

Uli liked working from the remote location in San Marco. It's located on a small strip in an upscale neighborhood. This helped to bring in top clients. And, the proximity of the office is within walking distance.

A small lamp on the corner of the desk provided the office's only light. He slowly rocked in the black leather, high-back office chair. The dark grey sweater hung behind him on the valet beside a pewter green jacket. In the corner, a six-foot grandfather clock confirmed the time.

"Eleven forty-seven. Two hours and forty-seven minutes late." He said to no one, as he pounded his fist on the desk.

With each passing second, the tick tock from the corner eclipsed the deafening silence occupying the office.

Then three hard knocks across the door panel broke the silence. He surely thought the next words would be, "This is the police. Open up!" But nothing followed.

Bamm. Bamm. Babamm. The knocks pounded the door again.

"Vas!" Uli shouted. His voice was swollen heavy by his German accent that escaped only when his anger was beyond control. "What?" He shouted, again.

"It's Seymour!" The man said, as he walked in from the hallway.

"You're late. And I mean really late. You smell just like that Orange."

"Well, if I am going to smoke, I might as well smoke quality. That cheap weed gives me a headache. Listen, Uli. You aren't my only client or my only appointment."

"What did you say, Seymour?" Uli was as hot as fish grease. "Before I made you my business partner, you were on the streets with no appointments and no clients!"

"Yeah," Seymour grumbled and twisted the toothpick between his clinched teeth. He removed it slowly and pointed at Uli. "But let's not forget, my neck is the only one out there. Not yours." He walked over to the chair and swung his feet on top of the desk. "See, Uli, I think it's time we talk about a raise."

"A raise!"

"Yep. A raise. You sit here in this big ole cozy office in your white-collar job while I'm the one taking all the risk." He rubbed the dust off the leg of his black, carpenter jeans and pulled a cigar from the leg pocket. "I get caught doing your dirty work. I go to jail. I'm all by myself, and on the other hand, you are untouchable. It's raise time." He lifted the cigar to his mouth and sparked a cheap lighter.

"Put that cigar out. Nobody smokes in here, and I do mean nobody. I don't care who you are or what you do," Uli said. Seymour smiled as he used the bottom of his shoe to put the cigar out.

"Now, let me get this straight," Uli said, feeling powerful. "I take you off the streets, put money in your pocket, make you a partner in exchange for the risk you take, and you tell me that's not enough?"

Seymour nodded decidedly.

"Okay, Mr. Seymour. You're right. I didn't think about it the way you are thinking. The risk factor should be taken into account."

In a tone too eerie for the moment, Uli's thick accent stretched the words "should be taken" and totally blended them with "into account" that Seymour turned towards him and stared. Fear flashed in his dark eyes and then vanished before Uli could notice.

"I know you're a fair man." Seymour said quickly, but Uli turned his back and slid on his pewter green jacket.

"There's a party I should have been at hours ago but I need to make a run out to Heckscher Drive first. How 'bout following me there?" He checked the inside pocket of his jacket and patted it with a little affection. His smile at Seymour was unusual but not alarming. With a slight chuckle, Uli said, "I'll put something in your pocket for all your trouble."

The two men walked out and Seymour opened the door to his green 2001 Honda Civic with the paint peeling off the hood.

"Uli, since you're in a giving mood do you think you could think about furnishing me with a work vehicle?" He asked as Uli opened the door to his three-day-old, 6.3 AMG Mercedes Benz. With a look of an Egyptian cobra, Uli slowly nodded.

Uli loved the feel of speed under his foot as he took the roundabout as fast as he could. He noticed how the two concrete lion statues in the center of the roundabout looked impressed. He waited a mile up the road for Seymour to catch up.

The two took 95 South in the direction of Heckscher Drive. When they came to the zoo exit, Uli got off and Seymour followed. Uli hit the gas once again. Seymour did the same this time in hopes of staying close. After coming out of the last turns, Seymour flashed his lights for Uli.

"Damn! Not here!" Uli turned around. "What's wrong?"

"I think I am going to need a ride home. This car is on its last leg."

"What?" Uli questioned. "Come on, Seymour, all the money I pay you, and you can't get a decent ride? Stop smoking that crap and having all the parties you throw for your street homies and maybe you can have quality, other than weed."

"I don't tell you how to run your life and you don't tell me how to run mine, White Collar."

"Okay, Seymour. I don't want to argue with you put your flashers on and I will ride behind you with my flashers on until we get to the gas station. Then I can take you where you need to go and maybe make the party." About half a mile later, they came to a point where Heckscher Drive runs along the St. John River when Seymour's car started smoking.

"That piece of crap isn't going to make it to the gas station." He said and adjusted the car stereo's playlist to listen to "Moonlight Sonata" by Ludwig van Beethoven. Uli drove beside Seymour and gestured for him to pull over. Both cars moved near the water to clear the flow of traffic. A cruise ship docked about a mile away at the pier. The moon and the ship provided the only light. As Beethoven continued behind him, Uli walked over to the passenger's side of the Honda.

"I think I see what's wrong with your car, Seymour, let me show you." Uli said, as he pointed to the passenger's tire. Seymour walked around the car and turned to look in the direction that Uli pointed. "I don't see anything." He said, turning around to face Uli.

Uli stood inches in front of Seymour, looking him directly in his eyes. "I haven't always been a white collar type of guy," he said as he thrust the Boker knife into Seymour's chest at the center of his pocket. He stabbed Seymour repeatedly until he fell. The knife was designed to go in easy but rip flesh with each exit. With one last jab, he let the knife remain in Seymour's chest. "That's a little something to put in your pocket," Uli whispered as Seymour collapsed.

Uli checked to see if any cars were approaching before he continued, nothing was in sight. He popped the trunk of his Mercedes and quickly pulled out two neatly rolled plastic garbage bags. He stepped into them one by one, covering the legs of his pants.

He walked back to Seymour whose body shook. His throat gurgling. Uli checked his watch. *Damn, one fifty-seven.* Then he scanned the terminal and highway for onlookers before he knelt to move the body. He turned the knife twice in Seymour's chest before yanking it out a final time. He grabbed the body at the ankles and dragged it ten yards into the retreating vacuum of waves as the puissant tide did the rest.

"How bout that for a raise, Mr. Seymour?" He said watching the body sink out of sight in the river. He allowed the water to wash clean the knife.

He stood by Seymour's car humming the crescendos of Beethoven with his eyes closed. He breathed in the night air and returned to the trunk of his Mercedes. He removed the bags from his legs and found a heavy-duty, black construction bag in the trunk to hold the soiled trash. He dried the knife with the bag and slid it back into his jacket pocket.

He got in the car, humming, with a smile.

He turned up the radio and drove home for the easy thirty-minute, Sunday drive.

CHAPTER FIVE

~~~~~~

Ava stretched her arm out of the water with everything she had left, ending a grueling pace. She touched the marble wall for her sixtieth lap. She pulled her face out of the water and took in a colossal gasp. Shaking from exhaustion, she barely held on to the edge of the pool with her forearm. She used her right hand to quickly remove her goggles. She spun around to check her time. The digital clock that hung fifty meters across the lap pool showed 28:40.

A slight smile emerged as she thought back many years ago to the exact day her grandfather barked out orders to the grounds crew as they installed the pool.

"This has to be the official length! There's nothing too good for my granddaughter. She's trying out for her high school swim team. When she's training, I want her to be completely conditioned for the official distance."

On that day, a teenaged Ava watched Opa from the third floor balcony. When he noticed her, he gave her a quick wave with a proud smile. Then, he said to no one in particular, "See, there is my little Kristin Otto. She, too, can bring home six gold medals in the Olympics. That German blood runs strong through her veins."

Ava stood there and smiled at being compared to a great athlete at the pinnacle of their career.

The memory caused Ava to chuckle as she lifted herself out of the pool. Her long torso and legs took forever to completely emerge from the pool. Steam rose from her body. She glistened with sweat. Her bottom jaw and arms trembled at the temperature change. The early morning sunlight offered little warmth.

"Ava! Ava. Ava!"

Her trance broke once she noticed Gertrude holding the parka open like a matador. Ava quickly tipped-toed into the out-stretched parka.

"You got to bend down, girl, you know I'm not that tall."

Gertrude wrapped the parka around Ava.

"I didn't see you when you came out," Ava admitted.

"I know you didn't. Sweat and steam popping off of you, reminding me of the days Poppa would let me dry off the horses after he used his special soap. They were all cleaned and smelling fresh. Steam still rose from their body because they ran so hard at the Kentucky Derby," Gertrude said quickly. "What are you doing, child? Are you trying to catch a death of pneumonia? I know the pool is heated I get that. But when you get out, you don't have anything. I'll be the one nursing you back to health, and that doesn't make a bit of sense when it could all be avoided, with a parka. But I guess that's just too much like right!" Gertrude said as the two walked to the main house with Ava wrapped in the warm parka.

"I'm thirty-six years old, without child, and I have to keep gravity at bay. I have to be ready for the day I take the pregnancy test and it comes back positive. So staying dedicated to fitness is a must," Ava tried to argue.

Gertrude raised her right eyebrow, tilted her head to the side, and then slowly folded her arms. "Young lady, if you died from pneumonia, there won't be any you. There won't be a child. There won't be anything. Besides, I thought that this was why you bought that fitness center."

"That was part of the reason," Ava admitted. "It was also a good business venture. Remember, I am my grandfather's granddaughter. When I found out Sheila was having financial difficulty and had to sell, I looked at the numbers and knew it was a good deal. She was making enough money. The funds were just mismanaged. She fell too far behind. So, I hired her as the manager. I killed two birds with one stone: I kept all my workout buddies and made a great investment without sacrificing my work."

"Okay. Ava, let's talk. I looked at the thermostat and it read thirty-three degrees outside. Then, I looked again and what did I see? I saw you in the pool, outside, under an open sky." Gertrude smacked her lips and shook her head. "Yes, you are Opa's granddaughter but I must say you are definitely Silka's daughter, too. We could always find your mother in the pool especially when she wanted to let off steam even if it was in the dead of winter. If the pool was heated, it didn't matter how cold it was outside, she would head to the pool at M.I.T."

Gertrude far surpassed the title of domestic help a longtime ago. She was Silka's very best friend. "Child, why don't you go upstairs and get out of that wet stuff? I'll have something nice and warm for you when you get down here. And maybe then you will tell me what's on your mind."

The two walked inside. Gertrude took the wet towels into the mudroom while Ava walked upstairs to shower and dress.

~~~~~~

Ava came downstairs in a white robe and sat in the most comfortable chair in the kitchen, while she watched the medical channel. She folded her long legs in a yoga sitting position and slowly sipped the warm, Keelung black tea Gertrude placed before her. She glazed at the television but seemed to look through it instead. Gertrude stood beside her for a minute then returned to the kitchen.

"Honestly, Auntie Gert. There's nothing wrong."

"Ummm, Ava," she practically sang the words before taking an exaggerated breath. "Okay, dear. I'm here when you need me."

Gertrude let the silence between them stay momentarily before offering more lively energy. She chuckled. "Ava. I don't know how you fold those mile-long legs of yours and sit so comfortably like that. But you always have especially when you had something heavy on your mind." Ava caught the hint.

"Okay, Auntie Gert. I have to be honest. I am pissed. I don't believe this crap," she said through gritted teeth as she pounded her forefinger on the table.

"Okay. Let it out."

"Do you know Uli didn't show up for Opa's birthday party?"

"No."

"Yes," Ava said and let out a moan trapped deep in her throat.

"Maybe he had to work," Gertrude said, trying to be conciliatory.

"That's the excuse I gave Opa."

Uli whistled as he strutted into the kitchen. Every strand of his black hair was in place. This morning he wore a matching embroidered, silk, green pajama and robe set. Uli and Ava had known each other since middle school. They'd been married now for sixteen years. As with all marriages, theirs had issues, spoken and unspoken. "Morning, Gertrude," he said.

"Morning, Mr. Ullrich," she responded, making it a point to leave them alone to talk.

"Morning, Ava." He kissed the top of her head before taking the newspapers off the kitchen counter. The family read a collection of papers regularly including the Wall Street Journal, Florida Times-Union, Florida Star, Business Wire, and Financial Times. Uli flipped through the papers to confirm that they were all there. He nodded.

"You know you missed Opa's ninetieth birthday party last night, and I had to cover for you, again," Ava said to his back as he walked to the other side of the dinner table.

"Uli, you make things so difficult. You make it hard at times to be Mrs. Ullrich Kärcher." She snapped out her name in a way that sounded snide and sarcastic. "I've been doing this supportive wife thing for a while now. Waiting for your career to take off and now we are there. We've been there. You're the vice president, for Heaven's sake! All I asked you to do was just show up for Opa's party!"

Uli closed his eyes and placed his left hand on his forehead as he slowly massaged it with his fingertips. "Man. That was last night? I knew I was supposed to be somewhere. I just got caught up finishing a business deal."

"You know Opa asked about you. I told him you were working like always."

"You told him the truth. I was at the office up until the early morning. He knows, as well as you know, there is a six-hour time difference between Europe and here." Uli reached over and placed his hand on Ava's "I'm truly sorry. I really wanted to be there."

"Opa turns ninety only once in his life, and you know he is the only family I have in Jacksonville."

With his hand still on hers, he gently squeezed. "I know. He and Oma raised you after your parents died in the car accident. But I am family, too."

"Uli. I didn't mean it that way! Of course you're family. I was just talking about Opa. We lost Oma last year, so now he needs us more than ever. We are all he has now."

"What happen to Gertrude? Where's my coffee?" They looked around the open room into the kitchen. Windows as tall as the walls opened out to the beautiful veranda where hummingbirds and butterflies gathered during the spring. Gertrude could be seen in the distance. Ava sighed, "Oh. I'll get your coffee."

He watched her tinker with the gold-trimmed cup and noticed the muscles etched in her forearm. Her tan was naturally beautiful; she made little to no effort to keep it up.

"You know what I missed most about you not being at the party?" She asked balancing the cup and saucer. "I missed you and me. I love dancing close to you, being in your arms, laughing while you hold me. I want us to start a family. I can hear my biological clock ticking so loudly I can't sleep at night, especially when I am home alone. Our bed is so cold in the middle of the night while you're cutting deals. I miss your warm body next to mine." She placed his coffee on the lace mat in front of him. He nodded his thanks.

"Uli, intimacy is almost nonexistent between us," She sighed. "You live at the office. I know you say you're preparing the future. But if we won't have anyone to leave it to, now what good is it?"

She returned to her seat and fingered the rim of her juice glass as he spoke. "You know I have certain goals, and the only way I can make it is to keep working to get there."

"Uli. We own the company. When Opa joins Oma we are the C.E.Os then."

He slammed his fist on the dining table and the orange from Ava's glass spilled. She quickly grabbed a cloth napkin and wiped it up.

"Your Opa doesn't like *me*; he never did. He just puts up with me because I am married to you."

Walking back to the table from the faucet, Ava said, "That's not true."

"WE! WON'T OWN ANYTHING!," Uli yelled to her surprise. He cleared his throat and lowered his tone. "If your Opa trusted me, I would be C.E.O now. Do you know he has superseded me twice on some important decisions just last week? Even after all I have done for Star Real Estate!"

"According to Sotheby's International Realty we have stayed in the top three real estate rankings in the world markets since he started this firm in the '50s. You were just moving a little too fast for him. On those particular projects, he wanted a little more time to think. He is grateful for what you have done for the firm—he even said that at the last board meeting, Uli." Ava defended.

She paused and sighed. "Remember you started at the bottom. And each and every time, Opa has shown his gratitude. Be it the purchases of the warehouses in the Bronx or the million-dollar residential development in Manhattan, Opa has backed you." She hammered her index finger on the dining table with three quick blows.

"Have you forgotten when the board was totally against the Chelsea New York project? Opa stood in unwavering support of all your recommendations." She shook her head. "I told him you believed with all your heart that Chelsea was going to be great for the company. You remember. He got behind you one hundred percent and the deal moved forward exactly how you orchestrated."

"Yes, you're right, Ava. That is exactly what I am talking about. I am depending on the old man to give the okay or, at the very least, his blessing. I have done enough developments to be further than where I am in this firm."

"You are the vice president! Next step is C.E.O."

"Ava, I spoke with your Opa," Uli sneered. "He informed me that I will be the C.E.O but the next step for you will be president. You will have the power to veto and fire anyone. His position is that his bloodline will always be the lead voice." Uli paused and stared coldly into Ava's eyes. She watched closely as his iris shrank and pupils darken during the five seconds they held each other's stare. Uli stood to walk away but decided to sit back down to say, "His lawyers have an iron-clad directive that if you try to supersede his wishes, the company will be sold and the money goes to that Clara mission place. It's the only charity listed in his will."

"You don't have to worry about your decisions being vetoed by me. Firing? That is the least of your worries when it comes to me. We are a team: Mr. and Mrs. Ullrich Kärcher. And we are joint heirs," Ava tried to sound convincing.

"He would never tell you, Ava, you're his baby doll treasure, always on the outside and always benefiting, but when the will is read, it will be law."

Uli gestured for her to come to him. She walked over to straddle him. With her back pressed against the table and her thighs pushed against his, she looked directly into his green eyes as he spoke, "I need to earn all the capital necessary to live the right way. I don't want to live by anyone else's ultimatum. I don't want to remain in his mansion, with his help, and under his authority. When you live like that, things can be taken away from you in a split second."

"I know." She nodded and closed her eyes as she placed a soft wet kiss on his lips. "We aren't often in this passionate situation. I like this. I want to take full advantage of this and turn up the heat." She gave him a sly smile. "Now that I know what your plans are for us, I will be more understanding of that, I promise. All I ask is that you set aside just a little time for us. I am getting to the point of needing to feel the kicks of a baby growing in my belly. I feel you will make a great dad."

A smile took over his face. "You are absolutely right in your prediction, Madam. I will make it an early day at the office tonight. We

will have a romantic dinner and practice on getting us pregnant."
He paused and gave her a slow soft kiss. "I tell you what, make dinner reservations for this evening, and I will join you. Leave all the
particulars with the Ms. Ruth. I promise, I will be there, and I won't
be one second late."

CHAPTER SIX

~~~~~~

Ava drove home humming and singing along with the radio in her convertible AMG SL6.5 As she swerved through the circle driveway in front of the villa, she spotted Roger and Opa entering the house. She quickly parked the car and ran to catch Opa.

"Opa!"

"How's my favorite girl in the world?" He said as he kissed her on the cheek.

"I'm fine, Opa. How was your day?" His smiled told her he had a great day. She took his arm from Roger and began guiding him through the massive oak doors.

"I talked with Uli earlier today, and he told me the craziest thing in the world. He said he would never be president and I would get that title instead. He said the closest he could get would be C.E.O." She waited for Opa's response, but he offered none. Roger turned around to begin moving both cars to the garage.

"Opa, do you really think that is fair to him after he has worked his way up the ladder?"

"Ava. Come with me." He directed.

Opa and Ava entered the front of the home and walked through the foyer, over to the right wing of the villa where Opa lived. "Smells like Gertrude's soul food night." Opa said as they both inhaled the deep aroma of mixed greens, kale, okra, and onions. They walked in the direction of Opa's office.

Gertrude came to the door, "Dinner will be ready in fifteen minutes."

"Thanks, Gertrude. We won't be long. Would you mind closing the door behind you?"

"No, sir." Gertrude closed the door.

"Uli is absolutely right. He will never sit at the head of this company. The head of this company is always going to be the smartest executive, a courageous leader, and a shrewd developer. And they will always have my blood running through their veins." His voice was uncommonly loud. "That's not Uli. Ava, you are the next leader of this empire!" He said with something close to rage in his eyes.

"Oh, Opa."

"Opa nothing! Ava, when is enough going to be enough? We don't owe the Kärchers anything! I don't know how your Oma explained it to you. But, she might have missed a few things because she wanted to help everyone connected to mission homes and their families. Nothing would have made her happier than to go back to the way life was before Hitler." He said as he sat behind his desk. "We were three close families and things finally got to the point to where we had to leave our land. Everyone had papers, everyone except your father's family because they weren't considered to be pure German. All three families bought homes the same day so we could be together, right next to each other. Our babies all played together; we all ate at each other's homes. Yes, Uli's grandfather had power in politics. So he had papers drawn which allowed him to leave."

Opa stopped talking while he twisted the cap from the carbonated water bottle and drank a sip. "When we started our company your father's family worked and sacrificed with us. When we came to America, we tried to make it work. Uli's family went another direction. Your Oma and I found a family to adopt Uli as an infant. They would eat over at the mission from time to time. As soon as we were able to, we took care of the family that adopted him."

Ava raised her head and had a look of disbelief.

"Yes. That's the complete story, and I know Oma didn't share it all with you. We found a family without a child and arranged for them to speak with Uli's parents before it became critical. Your Oma and I funded the entire thing. After the Great Depression, Uli's parents starved to death. Pride was their demise."

"Maybe I should tell him," she wept. "Or we could tell him together."

Opa came from behind the desk with his handkerchief and sat in front of Ava as he dried her tears. "No. It's too late. He has too much anger in his heart. I see the way he treats you. I don't see why you let him get away with it. Why do you dumb yourself down for him? When you two go out you don't even order your food. You keep quiet. I can not comprehend that. He seems to be angry at the world. Especially after the death of the only mother he had known."

"He blamed me for that, Opa."

"I know. And I am glad you did not allow it to stop you from being a great surgeon. On top of that you still use your business degree and your beautiful heart to build and maintain our legacy here in America and in Germany."

"How do you know I use it?"

"I might be old but I am not cold. The fitness center and most of those deals Uli brings to me you have dissected and perfected. The Chelsea project. That was you. You would brief him although you would never show him the spreadsheets and blueprints in your mysterious briefcase. Armer junge."

Ava smiled.

"Why would I not go to die intelligenteste person and make her the president? She is my seed. She is my blood. She is me fur immer!"

"Point taken, Opa."

CHAPTER SEVEN

~~~~~~

I f someone walked in here they would think I am crazy talking to myself."

You're not crazy, Calvin. I am here. I will be here with you as long as you need me.

"I see you as clear as the nose on my face," Calvin said to the image of Déjà sitting on the new, granite kitchen counter. He'd been talking to her for little more than an hour while he chopped onions, bell peppers, and tomatoes. "You're all on top of my counter with your legs folded..I never could tell how you could do that and stay that way for hours, studying, and tasting my cooking. I loved the way you indulged in my new dishes, licking your lips, and bouncing your knees. You encouraged every passion of mine."

The sound of the doorbell interrupted him. He turned off the faucet and grabbed a folded towel off the counter to dry his hands.

"Family's here."

Calvin, wait. You'll be fine. Someone is going to come into your life. Then you won't need me.

"Stop." He told her. After five years without her physically, Calvin had found comfort with his mind beset by hallucinations of a con-

KENNETH THOMAS SR

tinuous life with Déjà. He looked at his watch "Nineteen fifty," he said. A slight grin appeared at the corner of his mouth. He opened the front door with enthusiasm.

"If you're on time, you are late," he and his father said in unison as they shook hands, embracing into the one-arm man hug. The normally reserved retired Command Sergeant Major, who stood a shade over six feet, looked up into eyes he once looked down into.

"Okay, break it up, Hollaway. There are other people here to see Calvin. I gave birth to him; I should have been the first to get a hug anyway. Let me get a hug from my son, too," the elegant, tall woman said as she separated the two men.

"Your grandmother is here," she whispered in Calvin's ear, kissed his cheek, and backed away.

"Hello, Grandma." He bent down to kiss her on the forehead.

"Wa dey puttin' in ya food, child?" She asked with her strong Jamaican accent, patting his back a little too hard.

His grandfather was the last to greet him as they all enter the house. "Now this is how Sunday's supposed to smell!" His Poppy said. "Seems like you learned something from my girl and your momma. Because it smells just like her curry chicken up in here."

"If you think it smells like her cooking, Poppy, wait until it hits your taste buds." Calvin laughed. "I learned a lot from both these ladies. Déjà would say how blessed she was to have married her personal chef."

His father asked, "Should we take off our shoes? I would hate to mess up these beautiful floors."

"No, Dad. You all are fine. I'm so glad you could make it. I was thinking what better way to show off all the hard work I put into my home than with a wonderful Sunday dinner."

"This renovation took some time, son. But I must admit it turned out much better than I thought it would. These hardwood floors are

42

super shiny. Are they like this throughout the entire house?"

"Yes, sir."

"I got to tell you, son, these floors are like walking on a mirror."

"You like the floors, Sweet, and I like this high ceiling and the way our boy has decorated the place. Everything is in its place and so neat. It's just like our house," his mother said.

"Well, Mom, I guess that's what happens when you're raised by a sergeant major."

They all laughed.

"Me like da family look, child. All da pictures. Me like dis one here. Ya Papa and Déjà pinin' on ya rank." She pointed at the pictures on the table under the gigantic mirror.

"Yeah, Grandma. I like that one, too."

The aroma of curry chicken crept in the living room for the second time. Watery mouths and a severe case of growling stomachs took over the conversation completely.

"Man! Smell that? It went straight to the bottom of my stomach." Calvin said and quickly walked away. "Let me go check on the food. I'll be right back."

"Oh, no, you don't! Your grandmother and I are coming. We're going to see if you're doing everything right," said his mom.

"Okay. Dad, Poppy, can I get you two something to drink while I'm in there?"

His father replied. "Yeah, a cold beer for me."

Poppy agreed, "Yeah, that sounds nice; make it two."

They stood in the sitting room that was led into the dining room. The African decor was bold. Natural earth-toned colors and souvenirs Déjà and Calvin brought back from their honeymoon in Africa. From different angles on each wall hung a spear, a warrior's shield, and separate busts of a male and a female African. The dominate piece in the room was a three-by-five-foot oil painting of Déjà donning Kente attire and a traditional headrest that Calvin hung in the middle of the room. No one commented on the painting but they all took in its majesty and felt a lingering loneliness.

When the kitchen door swung back and forth, it released all the aroma dancing out of the boiling pots. Their salivating mouths now had to deal with overpowering scents of smoked turkey basking in collard greens along with the smell of spicy red beans and Jasmine rice.

The ladies were in awe the moment they entered the roomy kitchen. Even with an island in the center it was still spacious. Calvin had installed all top-of-the-line appliances.

The only way to satisfy their anticipation was for the women to do a quick taste test and confirm their suspicions. Both women grabbed wooden spoons and scooped a taste from each pot. His mother gave each dish a passing grade. "Calvin, you were paying attention when we had you in the kitchen. This meal is perfect if I must say so myself." His mother winked at him and continued, "Okay, son, your grandmother and I have it from here. Just take your dad and grandfather their beers and usher them to the table. We'll bring the food out."

Calvin wanted to keep everything uniformed, so he poured the beers into the wine glasses. He then called the gentlemen to their seats as the ladies came out wearing aprons and carrying dinner.

After everyone sat, Calvin asked, "Poppy, would you do the honors of blessing the food since you are the senior male?"

"I would be honored, but this is the first meal and the first acknowledgment to the Father of your home. I feel it is more appropriate if the first prayer comes from you."

Everyone bowed their heads as Calvin prayed.

After a few bites and praises to the chef, Calvin's mom asked, "So, son, why didn't you invite a young lady to be by your side and share this momentous occasion?"

"Mom. That's not right," Calvin mumbled through a mouth full of curry and rice.

His father quickly interjected. "Son, your mother is just concerned; we all are."

"I've tried. Honestly I have. But there is just no cure for this pain. My Déjà was what mom is to you. And what Grandma is to you, Poppy. When I lost her..." His words turned to mumbles, "There is simply no cure." He shook his head and looked down at his plate. "I have gone out on a few dates, and it's just been an empty, generic fix. It's nowhere near the strength I need to even attempt moving on and starting a new relationship. I am willing to accept that my days of being loved are gone."

No one responded. For the next three minutes, there were only sounds of forks tapping the china and periodic sips from glasses of beer, wine, and water.

Calvin restored the conversation. "Cheryl and I are having breakfast tomorrow morning before she leaves town." That news broke the tension and gave the all-clear sign as though a treaty had been signed and no more atomic bombs would be dropped.

"I want you to know your mother and I can't thank you enough for taking on her tuition expenses at Georgetown. We didn't know how we were going to afford that."

"It's no problem. I know the hard time you had putting me through college and that was while you were still active duty. You two deserved a break, and I needed to take that burden off your mind." Calvin said with more emotion than he wanted to share, "When you retired, I told Déjà about my plans. Then, we both put money aside for Cheryl. So when the death benefit came, I just finished what we'd committed to doing. Besides, I owed Cheryl that much for all the years I tormented her." Calvin laughed. "I must have decapitated every doll she ever had even though she was always so happy to see me walk through the door when I came home. I love my little sister."

"We love you so much. You know you're our favorite son, right?"

"Mom, I love you, too. But you do know I am Joyce and Will Hollaway's only son."

The energy from their laughter took over the dining room.

"How are things going on the docks?"

"Oh, Poppy, they are going great. Everyone still talks about you, like you're going to come out of retirement and become president again and run things like you did for twenty years."

His grandfather sat straight in his chair and took a sip of beer, "Son, those days are long gone now. With all the changes, everyone wants a shot at things especially now that there's very little backbreaking and manual labor. All the automation has taken over and made things a hell of a lot easier. But, I don't envy you young guys one bit. My time there has come and gone."

"I hear you, Poppy. Thanks for getting me on. The I.L.A. is just so different from being a U.S. Army Officer. I loved representing my country and paying for the price of freedom. That is something I will never change nor regret. In this new season in my life I am looking forward to seeing what's in store for me." Calvin said just before finishing his glass of water. "Landing this type of job was just the fix I needed, Poppy. It has great pay and the flexibility doesn't hurt, either. Oh, I didn't tell you. I was recently promoted to cruise terminal foreman and that has made things even sweeter."

Everyone raised their glasses and toasted to the news.

CHAPTER EIGHT

~~~~~~

The next morning, Calvin got up and did what he does every morning: wake up without an alarm at 4:15am then roll out of bed onto his knees to pray and thank God for one more chance to do the right thing. While still on the floor, he rolls on his back and goes straight into his workout routine: pumping out five hundred push-ups and five hundred sit-ups, alternating both exercises until he reached his goal within an hour. Then, he heads straight for the shower. Everyday, he does the same routine. This time when he finished, he put on the cruise terminal uniform, a fit, light blue polo shirt, hugging his massive pecks. The polo was neatly tucked into his pants that also outlined his tapered physique.

Calvin learned quickly that sexiness sells at the cruise terminal, and he made certain he maintained a well-sculptured, well-kept body and soul. The ladies tipped well. Even some of the men—especially the flamboyant ones—respected a guy who worked out. He walked pass the hall mirror and gave himself an approving smile before heading to the kitchen to see if Déjà was there. *She's not.* He had to remind himself—again. He took a deep breath and listened to the piano music coming from the house speakers. *I miss you.* He said within himself. *I've got to start over. This isn't healthy any more.* He closed his eyes slowly and breathed as deeply as he could until the pains in his chest finally stopped. He knew healing would soon come, but for now, he had to focus on Cheryl and keeping worries away from his parents.

He wrote a checklist to make sure he wouldn't forget anything.

- hire crew
- meet Cheryl for breakfast
- give her the envelope with both checks. *Are they both in there? Six months' mortgage payment for the condo and her last tuition payment. I can't wait to see her graduate. I am so proud of my little baby doll. Oh yeah, I almost forgot, better write this down, too.*
- Stop by the nursery

~~~~~~

After hiring a new crew from the union hall, he rushed to the east side of Jacksonville to meet Cheryl at his favorite breakfast spot on 6th and Walnut streets. Breakfast in a Cup was a quaint little bistro trapped in a time warp with all types of memorabilia from the '30s and '40s. He loved the three-foot statue of Betty Boop holding a tray of Royal Crown Cola, standing on the cashier's counter and watching the entrance.

He opened the door and allowed a beautiful woman to walk out. Two steps through the door, she stopped abruptly and said, "You are one gorgeous Black man! Your skin is so deep and dark and smooth like steel!"

"Thank you for the compliment." He smiled.

"My gawd! Your teeth! They are so straight and white! Looks like you brush them at least five times a day. I love a man with good dental hygiene and fresh breath."

He smiled again and gestured for her to come out as he held the door. She walked slowly pass him, looking him up and down.

"Umm-um. You are such a gentleman, too," was the last thing Calvin heard her say. He dipped his head a little to clear the doorway.

"Mark! What's up? Let me get two--"

"Calvin!" A voice rang out from the dining area, interrupting him. "I already have them here." He peeked around the door and saw Cheryl sitting at a picnic table in the dining room.

"Well. Well. Well. I finally meet the lady in your life," Mark said while placing his hand on his hips.

He looked Cheryl up and down and asked, "How tall are you?"

Before Cheryl could answer Mark gave his assessment. "Pecan tan beauty, you're about five-foot-nine."

"Thank you. But I'm five-ten."

"Mark. This is my younger sister. She's studying law at Georgetown University. She's never made a B in her entire matriculation, not in any capacity."

"Oh, your sister?" He asked as he extended his hand out to shake Cheryl's. "So there is still hope for me?"

"No. Mark."

"Why? Because I'm white?"

"No. Mark." He said shaking his head. Everyone laughed.

"I know he's straight but I just love messing with your brother. He's such a nice guy," Mark said in a half whisper.

"It was nice meeting you." Cheryl said as Mark placed their food on the table.

"Cheryl."

"What?"

"Who paid for this?" Calvin asked as he stirred his grits, eggs, and cheese in the bowl.

"I did, silly." She answered with a smile.

"Are you sure you're that poor little college student?"

"Yes. I still am. I just had a few dollars left from what you gave me last month." She said, holding back her laughter. He watched the smile on her face, revealing her deep dimples. She was still a baby doll. Tough as nails. Brilliant beyond his imagination, but still his fragile baby doll.

"Oh, okay. Well, let me see those grades."

She slid the gray envelope with Hoyas stenciled on it across the table to him.

"Not bad, Sis. Not bad at all," He said with a slight smile. It quickly disappeared when he asked, "Why's this criminal law class here again? I thought we agreed we were only going to concentrate on real estate law. That's where the money is, Cheryl."

Cheryl softly spoke. "Calvin, look at me. Criminal law is where young Blacks need help. The justice for us is simply not there. That's where I hear my calling. I love using the brain that God has given me to help others. I love all of the debating. I love how you must think quickly on your feet to win a case for your client. I love the satisfaction of it and helping innocent people by being their voice."

Calvin shakes his head and then places his hand on top of hers, "You're going to starve. The only types of criminals who would have any real cash would be drug dealers. That is definitely not the type of clientele we are trying to associate with. I want you safe and as far away from crime as possible. We don't have time for that kind of stuff. We need to concentrate on real estate law so our grades don't suffer."

She jerked her hand away. "*My* grades are at the top of the class. *We* don't have to worry about that," she said stressing the pronouns.

With a stern look Calvin replied "No. We had an agreement and I am not wasting money on that nonsense. So drop the criminal law stuff."

"Calvin."

"Cheryl. I'm not paying for it. I mean it. I don't want to see any more of this on your transcript ever again."

"Okay, Calvin," was her only reply.

"Cheryl. I just want you to get with the best real estate firm. Strong grades are the way to do it. No one can argue with a four-point-three G.P.A from Georgetown University and all the experience you have. Here's the check for the mortgage and your last semester." He gave her the envelopes.

"Thanks, Calvin. I know you want the best for me, and I won't let you or the family down." She put the checks in her bag and finished her juice. "I will be interviewing two more roommates now that the last semester is starting. They will take care of the mortgage." Calvin nodded.

They got up and walked outside. Calvin walked over to the passenger side and opened the door for Cheryl. She wanted to make a snide joke about Mr. Electric rolling in his new metallic 85D series Tesla but she kept it to herself. They both struggled to calm down on the ride to the airport. Just before he came to a complete stop at the sidewalk check-in area, Calvin broke the tension. "I love you, Sis. Go ahead study what makes you happy. Just do it well." He quickly wiped the single teardrop away hoping Cheryl didn't see it.

"I love you, too, Bro." He got out and opened her door and she hugged him and whispered in his ear. "I saw that, Mr. Softy." He smiled and quickly pushed her away. "Okay, Sis. Have a safe flight back to D.C. I need to stop by the shop and move a few things for momma. You know Pop's too proud to ask for help, so I am supposed to be just stopping by and she'll take it from there."

"Okay. Tell them I will call when I get back to the condo. The two hugged. She kissed him again on the cheek before he got into the car and drove away.

CHAPTER NINE

~~~~~~

Calvin walked into Hollaway's Haven, the family nursery and flower shop. Hanging high behind the counter, a colorful sign instructed, "Enjoy Your Flowers On This Side." The quaint, little storehouse connected to a massive green house in the rear. This was the slice of heaven where people traveled from across Florida and Georgia to purchase fresh flowers. It was located on the east side of Jacksonville in an area where African Americans only came for domestic duties. Now, it was owned by the Hollaways.

"What's up, family?" Calvin announced walking into the Haven. He kissed his momma and grandma. With a firm handshake and a one-arm man hug, he greeted his dad.

"Hey, Pop. I just left your favorite daughter and got her to the airport. You know Cheryl has to be the most stubborn child you have ever had! She is so set on this criminal law. I think it would be just a waste of hard-earned cash."

"Joyce, do you recall a certain son of ours doing something similar?"

"As a matter of fact, Will, my love, I do." His parents laughed. "I think your little sister could give you a good run for your money, big brother. When you were her age, we tried our best to get you to go into finance; but, there was nothing we could do to change your mind from being an engineer," his mother admitted, "The next thing we knew you were an engineer flying to Kuwait for the United States Army."

"Okay. Okay. I see your point. Looks like you have both raised two strong-willed adults." Calvin looked around the warehouse and spotted his dad attempting to move a large sago palm on its side so he could roll the flowerpot. "So, Dad, what are you up to?"

"Just going to move a few things around now that your mother has this new batch of Bird of Paradise flowers. I don't know why she ordered so many of these plants." Calvin slapped his hands together and rubbed them one over the other a few times. "Let me give you a hand, Pop. I got a few minutes and a few lil' muscles. Besides that could take you all day by yourself." He walked over to his father who softened his voice to explain.

"Your mother has this ingenious idea to educate all of Florida and America on this flower and how it should be the replacement for roses!"

"Well, I think it looks too plain, Pops. Will she be successful with that?" Calvin whispered.

"So. That's what you think, son?" Mom said as she walked over to where the two were working.

"Momma, they just look so plain."

"Sure they do. They're closed, like with anything of worth, the prize is inside." She dipped both her hands in a bucket of water and grabbed one of the Bird of Paradise flowers at its tip. The second it opened, a masterpiece of bright red pedals peeked out, followed by breathtaking yellow, then a deep blue sea of pedals all being hidden in a single flower shaped like a crane. Pop and Calvin stood there in shock. "Okay, Momma, I stand corrected," Calvin said.

"Me too, Baby. How could I have questioned you?" He gave her a quick peck on the lips. After everything was placed where Mrs. Hollaway wanted, Grandma came into the greenhouse with the coldest lemonade in town. The moment Calvin sat down and took a sip, his grandmother sprung into action, "Me want to know wat you waitin' fur? When you gunna bring a nice lady friend?" She said.

Before he could get a good taste of the lemonade and respond, his dad chimed in right on cue. "You know, Grandma is right. I want to be a granddad someday. It's time to get back in the saddle. This is coming from a man's perspective." There was silence among them as they all took in the seriousness of his father's tone.

"There are going to be some lovely interns coming to the nursery later today. I have narrowed it down to two young ladies, and you know mother knows best."

If he didn't know better, he would have sworn this was all planned. "Wait! Wait! First of all, interns? Those are babies, twenty something. I am not trying to raise anybody's daughter!"

"You need young and fertile. We don't want anything going wrong in the delivery room."

"Mom. I am okay. I know what I am doing! I have so much to do. I am getting Cheryl through college, and I have other things that need my attention."

"Calvin," his mom said in that way that stops the world. He looked at her and there it was: that momma-has-something-to-say-look. He saw the glisten of a tear. Her voice told him she had this building up within her. "Déjà is-" Calvin stopped her. "Momma, don't do that!" He kissed her then kissed his grandmother who was standing next to him. "I guess no one was listening to me last night," he said. "I love you all, and I thank you all for being concern for me," he took out his keys. "I meant what I said, every single word of it. I don't want this to be a problem but it looks like it is. I have to go before I am late for work. I can't be the boss and late."

His father realized the push was too hard. "Okay, son, we just love you so much."

"I know, Pops." He left and headed for the cruise terminal.

CHAPTER TEN

~~~~~~

"O kay, Ava, out with it," Sheila demanded. "You look like you have some serious radiation issues going on here. Have you just returned from Chernobyl or something?" She giggled. "When you walked into the gym this morning you had the biggest smile we've ever seen on you. With a glow like that I'm wondering if we can stay in the gym with you without being quarantined!"

All seven of the women in Sheila's spin class noticed the unusual glow on Ava's face. "Can't a girl just be simply happy?" Ava asked.

"The look you have is something much more than mere happiness," Sheila replied. Laughter came along with nods.

"Well, if you nosey bunch of women must know. I have a date. A date with my husband. A date that should lead to me conceiving the most beautiful baby in the world! It's time, ladies!"

Applause and laughter came from everyone in the small workout classroom. Ava caught a glimpse of herself in the wall mirrors and quietly rubbed her stomach imagining a small baby bump to match the magic she felt glowing within her.

"Okay, so what are you going to wear?" Nicole asked.

Then Dara, "Are you two going dancing first?"

"Oh, I know the perfect motel!" Charlotte boasted. Everyone looked at her as if she's let out the most putrid gas.

"I can promise you we are not doing this in any motel. Our beautiful baby will not be conceived in a motel, Charlotte!"

Charlotte withdrew her suggestion. "Sorry I was just trying to help." They laughed.

"I need you to lock up this evening, Sheila, if you can," Ava said "I have so much to do to get ready. I want this evening to be perfect. I can't remember the last time we had a date."

"Yes, ma'am. This is your joint now. I'm just the manager. Whatever you need, consider it done," she said, giving the ladies a wink.

Ava and Sheila walked passed the yoga classes and laughed more. They had become good friends since the finances of the gym no longer burdened Sheila. She could just be Sheila.

Ava hugged her and said, "Wish me luck!"

~~~~~~

After leaving the Apple Store, Ava stopped at the BookMark on First Street to pickup a medical book on robotic surgery. She also purchased magazines on German architecture and design. As quickly as she could, she paid for the books and returned to the car.

"Okay, Roger, we have to go to Five Points in Riverside. Wolfgang says he has this to-die-for outfit in his boutique that I need to pickup."

"Yes ma'am."

When they arrived, Ava looked all around and saw only a few nice things but nothing to the level Wolfgang bragged about. He made a grand entrance, swinging his arms, and practically singing her name as he walked up. The two did a quick side-to-side kiss on both cheeks. "Darling! How are you and Uli?"

"We are fine. I don't see the outfit you were speaking of."

"Honey! It's in the rear. It's so hot it wouldn't last on the floor an hour." Wolfgang quickly sashayed away and returned with the perfect classy and sexy corral-colored dress that stopped conveniently mid-thigh. The modest opening in the front would show off the white pearl necklace Uli purchased three years ago from Tiffany's. The opening at the back ended at the top of her tailbone.

Every second she spent in the pool and each spin class were the currency of this view and it certainly did not come easily. "Next stop, the hair salon," she told Wolfgang.

She made a call she seldom makes.

"Hi, Judy, I know you don't have me on the books so I have to use your emergency booking policy."

"You know that's three times the normal price?"

"Yes. I know, but this is definitely worth it. Uli has cleared his schedule this evening and is taking me out on a date tonight. I need you bad!"

"When can you get here? No! Don't answer that, just be here in an hour. I can move everything around to fit you in. Bring what you're wearing tonight, and we will work from there."

"Oh, thank you. Thank you so much, Judy."

She got there in an hour and asked, "Can you give me something sexy? I'm looking for something irresistible!"

"Let me see what you have first," Judy said. She turned the dress around twice. "Oh, yeah. This is something else! I don't think you'll have any problem when he sees you in this dress! I have just the thing to top this off!"

Judy pulled Ava's blonde hair up in a classy ball and gave her two spiral bangs at both temples.

"This will allow you to show off those pearl earrings and the necklace and when you walk in front of him he can have a complete and unobstructed view of all your sizzle!"

The women laughed.

For a moment Ava was surprised by her own laughter. She hadn't laughed like this in months, maybe even a year. She secretly hoped it was a sign of more good days to come.

"I wish I had your figure, girl."

"If you promise to be more dedicated and start coming to Schwarz early in the morning, I will guarantee you a figure like this and I won't triple the price." Ava said and put the cash on the register counter where Judy pulled out a calendar and wrote Ava into the day's log.

"Okay, Ava, you have a deal."

After looking in the mirror one last time, she thanked Judy and dashed out to the car just as Roger returned.

When Ava got home she ran her bath as hot as she could stand, filling her claw-foot tub with vanilla oil. The six-foot tub was burgundy with bright white interior and silver claws. She dropped two blue tablets in the water to give her all the suds she needed. She grabbed the magazines and book and placed them on the floor beside the tub. Ava dipped her toe into the scorching water; she gently submerged the rest of body. After her body acclimated to the temperature she reached for her reading material to start relaxing.

~~~~~~

At precisely seven thirty, Roger opened the rear door to the black 6.3 Mercedes Benz sedan for Ava to leave for dinner. She sat comfortably and waited for him to get behind the wheel. "Do you have the itinerary?" She asked. Before Roger could answer, her door opened and Priscilla, her personal assistant, rushed in.

"Where did you book dinner? What time is the reservation?"

With a smile Priscilla replied, "Hold your horses you have plenty of time. Your reservation's for eight o'clock. I selected a new restaurant in the St. Johns Town Center called Brio. It's a quaint Tuscany grille. It means 'lively' in Italian. I checked it out this afternoon personally, right after we got off the phone. This is the most lively that I've seen you in a long time, so I think this place is appropriate. You're going to love it, trust me."

Priscilla gave her a quick kiss on the cheek and exited the car, yelling, "Have fun!"

Roger pulled in front of Brio and slowly stopped. She made a quick assessment of the outside.

Priscilla was spot on. This is a nice place. I love the bright yellow building and the touch of green trimming is tastefully done. Ava thought.

Roger opened her door and she walked on the green carpet to the entrance. The doorman greeted her. "Welcome to Brio."

She smiled and gave a slight nod.

The maitre d' addressed her, "Good evening ma'am. Welcome to Brio. Are you Mrs. Kärcher?"

"Good evening. Yes. We have reservations for two. My husband will be joining me shortly."

"Yes, ma'am. Follow me, please."

She immediately looked up at the forty-foot ceiling and noticed the Italian ballet and six rustic, large chandeliers hanging from the glass dormer. The designer had set the ambience perfectly.

White tulle fabrics were Brio's stellar amenities. The mesh material weaved into dramatic hills and valleys to reach each chandelier giving a beautiful risqué effect above. Ava smiled. The beautiful material brought her mind back to her days as a young ballerina wrapped in beautiful tutus.

Brio's ground floor was equally as impressive with white tablecloths, flowers, and soothing lamps. She thought of a development project where this could be replicated if not in her own home.

Maybe after the baby comes. She thought.

All the men were dressed in suits or jackets and ties. The women were elegantly dressed and tastefully accessorized with elegant jewelry and perfect makeup.

I can't wait for Uli to get here! We are going to fit in so well. This is going to be a wonderful night, topped off with great sex to end the evening. She smiled.

Fifteen minutes passed, and Uli had not arrived. Concern turned into unsettling. After twenty-five minutes, it turned into anxiety. At forty minutes, optimism was nearly completely gone. After an hour it was painfully obvious. The tear stains on her dress loudly whispered her pain. The waiter was sympathetic and gracious while walking her out of the dining area. When he helped her in the car, he said, "Have a safe trip home, ma'am."

~~~~~~

Uli arrived home just before sunrise. Ava's eyes were still puffy from the night of crying.

"I am so sorry, Ava. Time got away from me. I really meant to be there last night," he whispered.

He took her in his arms. With total reluctance, she cried. He apologized again and kissed her forehead and held her a little tighter.

"Why don't you say we get cleaned up and go do breakfast?"

She wiped her eyes. "I really don't want to go out to eat anywhere. I'll just get Gertrude to make us something here."

"I'll grab a quick shower and meet you downstairs, Ava."

"Okay."

Man I got to do something. And I got to do it big. Okay let me get this rose here, that's what I'll start off with. Uli entered with garden-fresh flowers in a large crystal vase. She accepted them and took a whiff. "Thank you. But it's going to take more than you offering me a vase of flowers grown by my own hand. Don't you think, Uli?"

"I know," he said halfheartedly. "I have more. Last night, I made the biggest deal I have ever made in my life! But this time, it's going to be a new venture. It has nothing to do with your Opa's company. I spent all night doing this deal, and I want you to know I owe it all to you. So raise your glass and I propose a toast to my Ava Kärcher."

She watched his eyes dance around the room then they landed on her, but he never allowed his eyes to meet hers. She slowly raised her glass of papaya juice to his and allowed them to touch.

"Let me tell you what that means," he said with the same intense excitement she carried last night. "We are going to Europe! The two of us are leaving for Europe next month this time. After business is done, I will take you to Paris, and you can shop on the Champs-Elysées until your heart is content."

"That is simply wonderful." Ava gave him her best Mrs. Kärcher beaming smile to push back the residue of last night's disappointment.

"So you have a month to get everything together, and it's going to be great! It will be a vacation along with a little business. Who could ask for anything more?"

"Uli, we really need this. I mean our marriage, our lives really need this. I am going to love being in Europe with you. And the quality time will be our deal sealer," she said. "I have to head to surgery. Will I see you here this evening at dinner?"

"Of course. Business is going to take a back seat until we get to Europe, no more late evenings."

CHAPTER ELEVEN

~~~~~~

Later that evening, Ava returned home and took a short shower after completing two surgeries. Even with the intense work of the day, Ava couldn't wait to prepare itineraries for the trip across the Atlantic Ocean. She thought the Paris, France shopping spree was a nice and thoughtful gesture, but her focus was on the opportunity to explore the eastern part of Europe. She particularly wanted to travel through Dresdner, the origin from whence Opa and Oma came. After a thirty-eight minute bubble bath and five minutes of stretching, Ava slid into a olive gown and robe set with matching slippers. She brushed through her hair and promised her tired body that she would work for two hours maximum. Carrying a hot cup of chamomile tea, Ava walked through the villa to Opa's quarters where she felt most comfortable. She'd spent most of her time on that side while Oma was alive. As a matter of fact, she was hoping to speak with Oma's spirit while she worked at Opa's solid oak desk. She tucked her long legs under her body as she balanced in the matching oak desk chair that rocked slightly under her shifting body. Handwritten notes were sprawled across the table as she scribbled more ideas and locations for the trip. *Guten Abend, child.*

"Oma. Guten Abend." Ava smiled and looked around the room, hoping the spirit stood in enough contrast so she could really see her grandmother, "Oma, guess what." She asked although she could not find her in the space.

What?

"Uli is taking me to Europe. It is my first trip there and of course I'm going to the east. I have to see everything."

I told you Uli would take you places.

"We're going to start with the Semperoper."

Good choice, child. Uli's father played there as a classical pianist. He was such a child prodigy.

"Then we will go to the Katholische Hofkirche."

That will be beautiful. Your Opa and I were married there.

"The last place we will go is Frauenkirche."

Great. That was your father's family church.

Opa never made the trip back to his homeland so no one else did either. No one really knew why he never wanted to return. There were several different speculations. One was it would be painful for him to see what was no longer there. Dresdner sustained heavy bombing by the Americans and the British where 2,431 tons of bombs were dropped on during World War I. Another speculation was Opa's distaste for Hitler's response to the country. Hitler promised to regain everything that was lost in WWI, but managed to gain and then lose even more of the country Opa called home. The last was Opa's embracement that his country would forever be remembered for the racism and war crimes.

Child, why two itineraries?

"One is if I must go alone while Uli must work. The second is if Uli wants or needs my help, and we are able to go together."

Good idea, child.

Before leaving the office, Ava booked the three-hour flight from

Paris, France to Prague with an hour stop in Frankfurt. She couldn't pass up the opportunity to visit two of the top ten most romantic cities in Europe on the same trip. The two would then rent a car and drive the hour and ten minutes to Dresden.

"I am going to see every artifact from Opa's and your time, Oma, especially now that they have all been restored to their original grandeur."

Although she didn't get a glimpse of Oma, she almost certainly felt Oma's presence fill the room until she walked through the long corridors back to her room. They would travel in sixteen short days.

CHAPTER TWELVE

~~~~~~

R oger finished packing the car and said to Ava, "We're ready to leave, Madam."

"Thank you, Roger. I will go tell Uli." Ava walked towards the door then quickly spun around with a smile. "Roger, I can't remember the last time I was this excited! Europe, here we come!" Ava walked down the long corridor of the east-ern most edge of the villa. Her arms swung by her side to the swift rhythms of Antoin Dvořák's Symphony No. 7 in D minor, playing through the villa's twenty-year-old sound system. Roger followed.

"Uli, everything is ready for us to leave."

"How do you know? Oh, I see," he said, looking in the direction of Roger. His eyes met Roger's hardened stare much like the type box-ers give one another just before their gloves touch. Uli stepped to pounce in Roger's direction when Ava cut in his path.

"You know you don't have to like me just respect the fact that you work for me!" Uli announced.

"I work for Master Lang." Roger said deliberately. "Not you."

"Okay, Uli, let's just get in the car," Ava whispered quickly and touched her husband's chest. To her surprise, his heart pounded under her hand. *Was he really this angry?* She thought. Uli noticed the look on her face and gently took her hand to lead her out of the room. Roger submitted and stepped aside to allow the couple to walk pass him and back to the car.

The drive to the airport was quiet. Roger's eyes followed the edge of the road to see the very tip of sunlight peeking slightly over the horizon. He smiled at its beauty, grateful for his life, and remembering the years he slept under the sun's warmth as a homeless teen. The airport wasn't a far drive, and they arrived quickly.

Uli directed Roger to stop in front of the Delta Airlines' sky cab where two men wearing sunglasses waited.

As they unloaded the vehicle, both men walked directly to Uli, shook his hand, and kissed him on both cheeks. They said nothing.

"This is my wife, Ava." Uli offered.

Both shook her hand gently and nodded.

"Are you ready?" Asked the guy with a long scar tracing the right side of his face. Purple stitching sewn across a deep cut raised on his cheek. He was too sinister to be handsome but the way he smiled in Ava's direction let her know he thought highly of himself.

Ava answered, "Yes, we are ready."

He pulled Uli to the side, and the three appeared to be negotiating. While Uli nodded yes, the ominous pair shook their heads and said "no."

"It's not going to be a good idea if you let her fly with us," let out the taller one. Uli relented.

Roger stood by the driver's door and watched the men. He didn't flinch. Opa admired that the most of him.

Uli walked back to Ava and said. "Ava. We're not going to be able to take you with us."

"What do you mean, Uli?"

"Well, they have informed me the flight has been overbooked."

"That's okay. We can catch the next flight."

"The next flight isn't until 9 p.m. Besides, they have secured three seats on this flight, and you won't be able to go."

"Honey, it's okay. I don't mind catching the later flight. Just give me the itinerary and the name of the hotel. I will catch up with you. I am a big girl. You don't have to hold my hand. I'll see you when you are done with work that evening."

"That won't be possible," Uli said sternly. "We are going to be busy the entire trip. There isn't going to be any free time."

"Let me get this straight," Ava said, shifting the weight of her luggage on her right shoulder. "Are you telling me you're going to be working around the clock? Are you telling me there is no time for me in your life, again? Uli, obviously you forgot about our little talk. I meant what I said—" before she could continue she saw the unmistakable silhouette of Oma near the entrance. She shook her head slowly and fanned her long fingers in a slow, downward wave, signaling for Ava to calm down.

Ava took a deep breath and nodded at the image, "Uli," she said through gritted teeth, "You make it so damn hard being your wife."

"Listen, Ava. I'll make it up to you."

"Last call for flight 318 for New York"

The two goons grabbed Uli's luggage and headed down the corridor. He hurried behind them. Roger bolted around the car with dilated eyes. Ava had no idea where Uli was going or what type of business he would be doing. She didn't know when she would talk to him again, but when she did, he would be getting a piece of her mind, a big piece.

When she turned her head, Roger stood inches from her nose. "How long?" He asked and grabbed the luggage from her shoulder. "How long, young lady, are you going to put up with him? If Master Lang knew this was going on, he would put a stop to this. That I can promise."

She looked toward the airport door. As quickly as Oma had appeared, she'd vanished again. Ava's tears raced down her cheeks. She didn't answer. She simply got into the back seat of the car.

Roger was right.

After weaving through the airport exits. Roger cleared his throat softly and said, "I am sorry, Madam Ava. I was out of line and it won't happen again. I promise."

"I am okay. Please take me to Schwarz." *This was much more than some romantic get away to Paris. This was the place where my family was educated. Those universities are still there today. The love of arts, the love of classical music, the love of opera, the love of humanity, all started generations before I was born in Dresdner. My Opa and my Oma and even my mother. This trip would've connected me to everything that is them. Everything that is us. To have this nitwit take this opportunity away is unacceptable. I should've made all the arrangements myself instead of trusting him. Again.*

Her thoughts flooded her and she was grateful to see the black lettering Schwarz above the entrance as Roger pulled up. *I'll always have this safe place and my friends.*

When she walked into the gym, she noticed luggage lined around the counter and an empty gym. No music played. No one was exercising and the place smelled like the janitorial staff had just cleaned the entire facility.

"Ava! What are you doing here?" Sheila asked, shocked. "We thought you were already on your way to Europe."

"My plans have been altered beyond my control," Ava spoke slowly. "Uli's business partners decided it wouldn't be a good idea for me to accompany them. And he agreed."

"What?" Sheila asked in disbelief. She knew this was the second time Uli had disappointed Ava in less than a month.

"Yes. So I am stuck here in the good old U.S. of A with nothing to do."

"I'm so sorry, Ava, we are going on a two-week cruise of the Caribbean. We knew you were going to be gone for a month, so we thought the timing was perfect." Sheila confessed.

Ava slowly nodded.

"Ava, don't look so sad," Sheila said. Her voice was somber, "Felicia agreed to manage the classes and close out until we returned. You can still take this time off for yourself."

"I don't have anyone here now that you all will be gone. No friends, no husband, nothing."

"I have a great idea, Ava! Why don't you come cruise with us," Sheila suggested.

"I couldn't do that, you all had your plans already. Don't feel sorry for me. I declined to head a group of foreign surgeons that will be observing our robotic surgery unit. I'll just recommit to that."

"That's no fun! All you do is work, and that's not good." Shelia checked her watch and gave Ava an awkward smile. It was time for them to leave. "Hey, how about Roger and I take you all to the cruise terminal. And when you all return, we will be there to pick you up. All I want in exchange are the juicy details of every second on the cruise!"

Sheila laughed and they all agreed.

When the car pulled up to the curb, a nice elderly porter approached them. "Welcome to the Jaxport. My name is Buttermilk. May I help you ladies with your luggage?"

"Yes." Sheila answered. "Yes you may, Mr. Buttermilk," she said a little too seductively for his liking. He called two porters to come over to help.

"Wow! Do you ladies see what I see?" Sheila asked. "If this is a sign of what we have coming, then I can't wait to get on the ship."

The four ladies looked across the bridge of the ship pass the porters who were headed their way. They spotted the eye candy Sheila was watching, "How tall do you think he is?"

Nicole said, "Oh, he is six-foot-six and he weighs about two hundred five pounds."

"How do you know all that from this distance?"

"When you are five-ten like me and Ava, you have to know these things from a distance." Ava simply smiled and helped Roger reposition the luggage. She didn't look in the direction of who was causing all the admiration.

"Okay, ladies, Roger and I will be here when you all return. Have all the fun you can stand and don't forget I get all the details when you get back!" Ava hugged and kissed each of them. She chuckled to herself, shook her head, and watched her best friends approach the porter.

"Hello, ladies. Welcome to the Jaxport. My name is Calvin Hollaway. How may I be of service to you ladies?"

"I was just wondering how tall are you?" Sheila asked.

"I am six-foot-six."

Nicole blew the fingertips on her right hand and then brushed them up and down her chest.

"May I ask how much do you weigh?" Sheila asked.

"Sure. I don't mind. I'm about two hundred and six pounds."

"I must be getting rusty. I was off by a pound," said Nicole.

"Then again, you might be right, I do feel a little lighter today," Calvin said with a smile. He gave Nicole a wink and walked away. The women laughed.

~~~~~~

On the ride home not a word was spoken between Roger and

Ava. When they arrived to the mansion, Roger unloaded the luggage and carried them to the foyer closet. "Madam, I will leave them here in case your travel plans change," he hinted, but Ava didn't respond. Gertrude looked puzzled at Roger who simply pointed at Ava and walked out.

Gertrude watched through the foyer windows as he got into the car and drove towards his quarters. She remembered when he first arrived at the house to work for the Langs. He had a wise old soul and a tiny body, now his body has caught up. Gertrude smiled. *Silka would be proud.*

Ava called into human resources at the hospital to prepare the paperwork for her to begin the monthlong assignment. At least the work would keep her intellectual stimulated and satisfied, since the rest of her body wouldn't be. On her way to her room, she walked to the bookshelf tucked in a corner by the curved staircase. She pulled Schwarz from the middle shelf. She rubbed red lace sleeves on the doll's shoulder and brushed backed the black yarn hair. For a moment, she looked into the doll's eyes as if she could will her to come to life, then gave her a gentle hug and carried the doll to her room.

Her walk was quiet and solemn. When she made it to her room, she silently prayed for a visit from Oma.

CHAPTER THIRTEEN

~~~~~~

Roger stood next to Ava. They waited in front of a Do Not Enter sign nailed to a single post that served as part of an invisible fence separating the port from the terminal. Passengers exited the ship, laughing and waving at waiting loved ones. The noise—so festive and alive—surrounded Ava and, for a moment, she felt a tinge of sadness. *I could've gone with them on this cruise.* She allowed the thought to pass through her and quickly replaced its void with great anticipation.

She watched each time the twelve-foot frosted glass sliding doors opened to allow more passengers to exit. She saw Shelia and Nicole behind several exiting passengers. Jubilation took over as she jumped up and down, waving to them. She ignored the Do Not Enter sign and weaved through the crowd to get to them.

Her excitement quickly disappeared as she noticed the man in front of Sheila. He wore a traditional Kente outfit and had just stepped in front of the women. Ava sensed something wasn't right. In that moment, he grabbed his chest and collapsed. The sliding doors closed once again. Ava heard screams and cries from behind the glass and she began running towards the fallen man.

A customs agent ran through the doors when they opened. "Is there doc—" Before he could get the next syllable out, Ava ran past him through the opened doors.

Calvin turned to lift the man when Ava whisked in front of him. Her scrubs made it clear she was a surgeon at the Mayo Clinic, and the determination across her face made it clear that she was ready. Ava squatted as low as she could next to the victim. She grabbed his left shoulder and the left side of his waist. She closed her eyes and tightened her grip. With everything she had exploding in her legs and back, she looked up to the ceiling, and pulled. In that one motion, she'd turned the victim flat on his back.

Calvin froze. Not only had this nimble woman managed to reposition a man who clearly was three times her weight, but she carried a scent that soothed through Calvin's body, reminding him that he was still 100 percent man. *That's Love in White by Creed.* Calvin could recognize it anywhere, though he hadn't smelled the fragrance in years.

For what seemed like hours but was only thirteen seconds, Calvin closed his eyes and breathed in the aroma of the woman he had loved. It was the only fragrance Déjà wore. He jerked his head and returned his focus to the crisis now on the ship. Time with Déjà would have to wait.

"Everyone get back! Back them up! Fellas, back them up! Let her go to work," Calvin barked out. The customs agents echoed the same orders as they pushed onlookers back and guided them away from Ava and the African. Their eyes remained on Ava as she worked feverishly to save the man's life.

"What's his name!" She demanded. "What's his name!"

A voice softly said, "Abou. Ah - boo."

Ava pumped his chest with the balls of her gripped hands. "Come on, Abou, Come on." She told him, softly. She kept her rhythm between pumping his chest, blowing air into his mouth, and pinching his nose. Very near exhaustion, she asked a young woman with a coat of brown skin more beautiful than Ava had ever seen. "Are you his wife?"

"Yahs," she said. Her eyes glazed with fear.

Still pumping Ava commanded, "Come, hold his nose and cover his mouth with your mouth like you saw me do, yes?"

"Yahs," Abou's wife said, kneeling to his face.

"I will tell you when to blow. We will save him," Ava declared.

Rescue showed up but Ava didn't move. She gestured towards Abou's wife with her head for them to relieve her. She was obviously exhausted and out of breath. Calvin caught the woman before she fell and wiped her face with a cool towel. He offered her a bottle of water, but never takes his eyes off of the timid doctor and her giant patient. Ava knew that the best chance of saving Abou relied on her getting a pulse.

After forty minutes of working alone a pulse is found. Abou's chest lifted on its own as he caught his breath. His eyes stayed closed. "He's ready! Take him out of here!" She demanded. "Move! Move!" Applause erupted throughout the terminal. The paramedics moved through the cheering crowd and loaded Abou in the ambulance. Calvin guided the wife to her husband. Ava signed paperwork and pulled his wife into the ambulance with them. The EMT sped off.

Calvin stood there, still smelling the Love in White.

Roger gathered Sheila, Nicole, Dara, and Caroline and headed to the hospital. After an hour of arriving, Ava comes out of the emergency room and is greeted by cheers and applause once again.

"How is he?" Sheila asked.

"He's recovering. He will be fine." Ava said calmly but it is obvious she is exhausted.

"Ava, I have so much respect for what you do now that I saw that with my own eyes!" Sheila said. They all chimed in agreement. "Yes, Madam Ava, that was impressive," Roger said. He had been standing at the door since they arrived.

"Thanks, everyone, but it's what I've been trained to do. It's what I've been born to do—save lives."

Ava reached down her scrub's top.

"Oh! No! It's gone!"

"What's gone?" Sheila asked.

"My lucky brooch from Germany. It's gone! It belonged to my mother. I had it on when my parents were killed in the accident. Oma said it was what kept me alive, and I should never lose it."

They checked the floor of the hospital entrance and Ava went back into the emergency corridors but returned with nothing.

After convincing her that he would look through the ambulance to find the brooch, Roger took Ava home. All she could think about in the shower was where the brooch could be.

I must have lost it at Jaxport. I looked all through the car. The ambulance would have informed me, Roger or even the crew if they had found it. I'll go by the terminal in the morning.

She tried to reassure herself but nothing worked. She tossed and turned the entire night with Schwarz looking over her from the dresser.

CHAPTER FOURTEEN

~~~~~~

Calvin stepped out of the shower and wrapped a black towel around his waist. Just before he began to brush his teeth, he felt Déjà's presence. He looked to his left and saw her sitting on the seat of the commode. "Thanks so much for being at the cruise terminal today. I don't know if I could have handled all that without you, Baby."

Calvin, what are you talking about? I wasn't at the terminal.

"Are you telling me that wasn't you? Déjà, I smelled you."

No. I wasn't with you at the terminal.

"I know what Love in White smells like. It was you."

I promise you, Baby. I wasn't there. Calvin began to feel less of her presence. *I have to go.*

"Wait," he said. "Déjà, please, wait." Calvin looked around but didn't sense or see her anywhere.

He stared in the mirror until he remembered that the fragrance came from the small doctor at the cruise terminal. He wondered how and why she would wear such an alluring, expensive fragrance to work, and why had she and it captivated him. For the first time in a long time, Calvin fell asleep thinking of a woman.

CHAPTER FIFTEEN

~~~~~~

After Calvin arrived at the cruise terminal, Buttermilk was the first to greet him as always. "Hey, boss, everything is dress right dress and ready for inspection."

Calvin smiled. "Great, Buttermilk, you would have been a great soldier if you didn't have that heart problem."

"You think so, Boss?"

"I know so. Let's walk the floor." After a few steps, they came across a dual-toned, heavy metal pendant. Calvin picked it up, and his entire body glowed starting at the smile across his face. "Buttermilk, do you know what this is?"

"No, Boss. What is it?"

"This is a great piece of Black history that turned into undeniable American history," he said and stared at the pendant that spanned the width of his palm. "See these gold horizontal wings and this vertical, silver airplane propeller in the center?"

"Yeah. It's a pin."

"Not just a pin. It's a Tuskegee Airmen insignia. The greatest boomer escort unit ever in the world."

"Why is it here on our floor, Boss?"

"I don't know. But you can be sure the owner will be back for this."

Buttermilk nodded in agreement. He watched Calvin search his small office until he found a small, white box to keep the pin. He handled it with such delicacy that Buttermilk said, "Boss. It's not gold."

"You're wrong. It is gold, Buttermilk," Calvin looked at the closed box and put it in his bag. "I will be back. I need to stop by my parents' nursery for a few."

"Okay, Bossman."

~~~~~~

Ava walked onto the cruise terminal.

"Welcome to Jaxport. My name is Buttermilk. May I help you?"

"I am looking for the person who is in charge," Ava said.

"I am since the boss isn't here."

"I lost an heirloom that has been in our family for many years. It was pinned to my scrubs and it must have popped off during all the excitement the other day. I was just too focused on saving your passenger, Dr. Abou Diallo, that I did not notice when or where it fell."

"Oh. You're the doctor that saved that African dude."

Ava smiled. "Yes."

"We didn't find no air loom. But, my bossman did find some golden airplane pin this morning, though."

Ava smiled again. "Yes! That's it! Where is he? Where is it?"

"He had to make a run. It's with him, too."

"Okay. May I leave my card? And will you have him call me?"

"I sure will, ma'am."

Ava placed the linen business card issued by the hospital in his hand along with a tip and walked to her car. Buttermilk opened his hand and saw a one hundred dollar bill and gave her a thumbs up even though she didn't notice it.

Buttermilk rushed to the office and called Calvin on his cell phone. "Hey, Boss. You were wrong about that thing you found. It's an air loom." Calvin chuckled. "Oh, really?"

"Yeah!" Buttermilk practically yelled into the phone, "And guess who it's for."

"Who, Buttermilk?"

"The doctor lady from yesterday!"

"What?"

"Yep! She just left here sporting that new AMG SL6.3 convertible Benz. Gave me a yard for the reward."

"You don't have it."

"But I know who do."

Calvin laughed out loud.

"Boss her number is 777-9311."

Calvin called the number and it went straight to voice mail. "This is Calvin Hollaway with the Jaxport Cruise. I am calling you about the pendant I found. You can reach me at the terminal when you are free."

Ava was never available during rounds. She always turned her phone off and sent all calls to voice mail. After she checked on her patients, she went to say hello to Abou. She knocked on his door.

"Enter," a woman said. Ava opened the door to see Abou laying in bed, dressed in traditional wear with deep shades of gold and green. The beautiful wife with a soft, strong accent said, "I am Nandi Diallo." She extended her hand out.

"My husband, Abou, is grateful for his life. As am I."

"You are welcome." The two women hugged. "Where are you from?"

"We come from Nigeria."

"He, too, is the heart doctor. I told him you worked forty minutes with bare hands for his life."

He smiled and reached to remove his oxygen mask. Both ladies stopped him. "No. Do not talk with me, sir," Ava said. "I only wanted to see how you were recovering." He offered a large smile and reached to hold Ava's hand. The room stayed quiet for a while as the new friends held hands. Ava looked at Abou as she spoke, "I will leave you two for now. I will be back to check on you." Nandi hugged Ava once again before she left the room.

Ava walked out of Abou's room with her head down. The next thing she knew, her face was buried in a man's chest. She lost her balance as she bounced off him.

Calvin caught her body inches from his. He immediately smelled the Love in White again. He savored it for a brief second and shifted her weight to balance her on her own feet.

Ava raised her head to look up into the hazel brown eyes of a smoothed-skin, chocolate Adonis with a chiseled face and a smile to live for.

"Dr. Kärcher?"

"Yes." She answered in surprise.

Noticing she was standing on her own, he released her and extended his hand. "I am Calvin Hollaway."

Ava placed her hand inside his hand and instantly felt like a little girl shaking hands with a celebrity crush.

"I work at the cruise terminal, and believe I have something that belongs to you."

She gasped, grabbed the brooch, and brought it to her lips in one motion. She looked at Calvin. "Oh. I am so sorry. I shouldn't have snatched it."

"Don't worry. You are fine. I am glad to return it to you."

Ava reached into her pocket and placed a reward in his hand.

"That won't be necessary."

"Nonsense. I thought I would never see my family's heirloom again. Please take this as my thanks. This would do me good." Calvin obliged her and placed the reward in his pocket without looking at it.

"Paging Dr. Kärcher. Paging Dr. Kärcher."

"Oh, that's me," Ava said pointed at the intercom above their head. "Thank you again." She rushed off after they shook hands for the final time. Her scent lingered in the space she'd left. Calvin looked around the corridors hoping Déjà would appear and explain the smell and its effect on him. But, she wasn't there.

CHAPTER SIXTEEN

~~~~~~

Calvin walked into his favorite restaurant, A1A Ale Works, in the beautiful city of St. Augustine. Downstairs was a noisy sports bar with people holding plastic cups and watching one of the four, fifty-two-inch screens blast different sporting events.

He walked up a flight of stairs and the noise from the downstairs crowd faded. Halfway up, the smooth sounds of jazz took over. He stepped into a large, open room where eighty percent of the area was illuminated by candlelight. Each table was decorated with a white cloth, silk napkins, and long-stemmed wine glasses and beautiful white roses that his mother's team carefully delivered every Tuesday before the dinner crowd arrived.

At the top of the stairs the maitre d' greeted him. "Good evening, Mr. Hollaway. Your usual table?"

"Yes. I wouldn't have it any other way, Alex. You do know that's the best view in town?"

"Yes, sir. I happen to feel the same way."

For Calvin, the perfect evening out meant the opportunity to combine his three passions: high fashion, fine dining, and great music. Since the music was pumped in by satellite, two out of three would have to be enough.

Tonight, he walked with more swag and vigor than normal, thanks to the newest addition to his suit collection. Calvin was a black Boss type of guy. But this evening he stepped out of his fashion comfort zone and anyone watching him walk could tell he was glad he did. He wore a charcoal grey, three-piece suit with light colored blocks, oxford white Boss shirt, and a red silk flower tie to add a touch of flair. He completed the ensemble with matching red socks and traditional black Boss shoes.

Calvin followed Avery toward the balcony when he abruptly stopped. "Dr. Kärcher?" He said.

"Damn! You sure clean up well," rushed out her mouth before she realized it.

"Well, thank you. You're not doing bad yourself, Doctor."

"I'm sorry. I didn't mean to say that."

"Don't worry. You're okay."

"That suit. Isn't it Boss Black?"

"Close. It's Hugo. My first attempt at the brand and I like it."

"Well. You already know how I feel." They both chuckled

"Uh, Calvin. What are you doing here?"

"This is my favorite restaurant here in St. Augustine." Calvin did a quick glance over his shoulder then around the room before he asked. "Are you here with someone, Dr. Kärcher?"

"Uh, no. And please call me Ava. Do a girl a favor and let me settle my debt. Join me for dinner, unless—" Her voiced trailed on to say, "—unless you are meeting someone." She quickly sipped from a wine glass, half full of papaya juice, three cherries, and a slice of lime. Calvin took a quick review of what was on the table: five short, celery sticks each one bitten off of, a large architectural rendering, four design magazines, sketches of six Schwarz logos, and a fitness catalog.

After recovering her pin, Calvin did have a few burning questions he wanted answered. Like, what was this young, affluent, white woman, doing with a Tuskegee Airman's wing pin? He knew the pin well. His Grand Uncle Bill kept his wing pin in the cabinet, right next to the china that was used only for Sunday dinners and for guests who followed the family home after a long repast. He was given the wing pin from Alexander Jefferson, the best pilot in the Tuskegee Airmen 332nd Fighter Group who registered twenty kills. Grand Uncle Bill was Alexander's aircraft mechanic at the time.

"There is no debt. You gave me a hundred-dollar tip."

"I know exactly what I gave you. That was no mistake."

Calvin could no longer restrain his curiosity. "I am not meeting anyone. So, yes, we can do dinner. But it's going to cost you some info," he said.

"Okay. Ask away," she said, shifting her weight on the heels of her left foot, which she had pulled comfortably under her body while she worked.

"That Tuskegee Airman's wing pin."

"Yes? Go on."

"How did you get it?"

"Well, that's a long story for a man standing," Ava said with a big smile. She gestured at the empty chair across from her. Calvin sat across from her and Avery handed him a menu before walking away.

Ava looked Calvin directly in his eyes and attempted to explain the worth she gave to the pin. "I have so much respect for people who defend the lives of others and protect other people's way of life. If I am to be completely honest, my respect for the African-American soldier is even greater."

Calvin looked at Ava with skepticism. "Hear me out," she said.

"These soldiers weren't allowed to participate in World War II. Only when the dire need arrived was it even made possible for them to fight. And the Tuskegee Airmen proved to be worthy and invincible!

"When our family was being extradited to the United States, a Colored, escort bomber saw this little girl, nervously being herded through the crowd. He stopped the woman with her—that was my Oma with my mother—and he asked how old the girl was, and she told him. He told Oma she was the same age as his daughter. He asked Oma if he could give her a gift. She agreed. Then, he took those wings off his jacket and gave them to my mother. The entire family was honored by that.

"Oma said my mother loved the golden bird he had given her so much that when she got older and started her family, she named me Ava. It means 'bird' in German. So, I have carried the pin, as a brooch, with me everywhere since the day my parents died.

"In the sixties, African Americans could fight but were still treated subpar in America. So when my auntie gave me the doll that looked like her, I cherished it. I even named my gym after my doll. It's called Schwarz. That means 'black'." She pointed at the page of logos but did not share it with him. Calvin acknowledged them and smiled.

"I see you have done your homework on the plight of our journey. I have much respect for that; not many would."

He heard a voice say, "Major Hollaway." Calvin turned his head toward the voice. He recognized Anthony instantly.

"It's Calvin, now that I'm in the civilian world." Calvin said standing from the chair. They shook hands and hugged like old friends.

"Okay, man. I understand. I just would like to express my condolence to you and your entire family," he said as he placed his hand on Calvin's right shoulder. "When I found out what happened to your wife, Déjà, it left me in shock. She was a hell of an officer, a hell of a surgeon! Hell, there wasn't anything she didn't do well!"

"Thank you," Calvin replied with puddled eyes. He quickly pulled himself together and introduced Anthony. "Ava, I would like to introduce you to the commanding officer and lead surgeon of my wife's last unit, Dr. Anthony Thiel," he said. Anthony extended his hand to Ava, and they shook. Mrs. Thiel walked up behind the men and slid her arm around their waists. "Anthony, no shoptalk tonight, it's my birthday," she said and pulled him away. The men shook hands again and Calvin returned to the table.

Ava breathed a deep sigh of relief and said, "So, you and your wife were soldiers?"

"I was an airborne ranger infantry officer. You would think my job was the more dangerous one; she was killed the second day of Desert Shield," he said motionless.

Ava watched his eyes.

Feeling compelled to tell her more, Calvin said, "Losing Déjà was the main reason why I am no longer in the military. I lost a lot the day she passed." He travelled through a roller coaster of emotions as he spoke his truth to Ava.

"I chose not to re-enlist, then I started this new career as a long-shoreman. I tried a few things before I settled on this. I worked in my parent's nursery. I even did a little stint renovating and reselling houses." He took a long drink of water.

"Tell me a little about the day and life of a longshoreman," she said hoping to dissolve the hurt in his eyes. She was also hinting at something deeper.

"Okay," he said. He was a little relieved that she had changed the subject so gently. "Since we are bearing our souls, I want you to know, I've never met with any passenger away from the cruise terminal, and I do mean never! Most of the ladies who go on these cruises alone are wives who are quality-time deprived. Most tell me their husbands are workaholics or have just lost interest in them and by that time they are all hands—horny octopuses!" At that Ava laughed holding her hand just above her cleavage, which he hadn't noticed until that moment. "They just want to make me their short-term paramour. I can't do that!" She laughed more. The thought that he had made this beautiful woman laugh awakened something inside of him. He listened to her laughter, mentally recording the sound, until she calmed herself.

"So, tell me what's your story." He interlocked his fingers and sat his hands on the table in front of him. Before she could start, the waiter came to the table, "May I take your orders?" Ava froze with the menu in her hand but stared directly at Calvin.

"Don't worry. Anything you choose, you're going to love," he assured her. "You go first." It took her a minute to decide on the angel hair salsa cruda with blackened shrimp, and Calvin chose the key lime shrimp and lobster.

When the waiter walked away, Ava picked up the conversation where they'd left it. "Well, I am a little different. When it comes to the work alcoholic spouse issue that would be moi. I originally purchased my favorite ladies-only gym where I work out as a business investment. The financials worked well. The girl talk was great and the stress release phenomenal," Ava chuckled and ate another bite of the celery stick. "For men and women, there's a lot of pressure and challenges when the opposite sex trains in the same gym, so we kept that issue out." She waited for Calvin to respond but he didn't.

"My family is a proud family of German ancestry," she continued. "My great grandparents were immigrants who came here with little, but are totally responsible for our family's affluence. German customs, family beliefs, and old habits are hard to break so things are pretty much the same as a mindset for my family," she admitted.

"If your family saw you here sitting with me, having dinner, would you be ostracized?" Calvin asked pointedly.

She tried to understand the look on his face. "Well, I don't know about that. I was talking about our work ethic. But to answer your question, they would not be happy." He didn't react.

"How about your story? You are certainly not a typical guy," she said after taking a sip of her papaya juice. "You have what some guys would consider paradise. You have women at your beck and call. And your reply is, 'I can't do that!'"

The waiter interrupted by placing their meals before them, "Will there be anything else?"

Ava shook her head.

"No that will be all," Calvin replied. He bowed his head and quickly blessed his food. When he looked at her, he noticed her lifting her head and making the sign of the cross across her breast.

"You may be right about other men seeing this as paradise. But the temporary flings aren't for me," he said. "I love being in love." Then he took in a fork loaded with creamed spinach. "That's a serious thing for me. If I am holding a woman in my arms, she is my world; so I don't have time for anything less or anyone else," Calvin said then paused. "Wait. Let me get this straight, as attractive a woman as you are there's no dating in your life?"

"Dating? As in out on a beautiful night, enjoying beautiful music, savoring a delicious meal, and being treated like a beautiful woman? Honestly? No. I can't remember the last time I've been on a date or anything resembling dating," she said with sarcasm.

The two went on to enjoy the rest of the meal. Calvin thought, *I can't believe I spilled my guts like that. I got to get out more. But, it sure feels good to have a beautiful woman sitting across the table. It's been su a long time.*

They both passed on having dessert and decided instead to each have a glass of strong, dark tea with honey that Ava ordered. After a short argument over who would pay the bill and allowing two flips of a coin to call a tie, Calvin said, "Ava, I want to thank you for dinner and a wonderful conversation."

"Did you really enjoy my company?"

He smiled and replied, "One thing you must know about me is I find honesty to be an honorable, endearing, and sometimes sexy trait. Honor and my word are what I've always had. So if I tell you something, it will be the truth." He stood up from the table and walked over to pull her chair.

"Calvin, I really enjoyed this time with you," she said, allowing him to guide her out of the chair. She collected her papers and books into a leather satchel. "I hate to end this but we both have early morning schedules. Thank you for your company."

They smiled, shook hands, and said their good byes.

CHAPTER SEVENTEEN

~~~~~~

On Uli's first day back at Star Real Estate, everyone was on pins and needles. His secretary offered no "good morning," no coffee, no "how was your trip," and no smile. The first words from her were dry and matter-of-fact. "Mr. Lang would like to see you in his office right this minute," she said.

The old man normally came in only for the most important staff issues. He rarely came to the office to meet anyone one-on-one. If he did, there were only two reasons: to promote an executive or to fire one. With the way things were going between Uli and Ava, Uli would have bet his money on the latter.

For nearly a minute, he stood outside the executive office contemplating all possible scenarios. He finally shook his head, shrugged once, and then knocked on the door.

"Ullrich. Come in, have a seat, welcome back. I would like to tell you about our plans to expand your idea of the European-style town centers. I shared the concept throughout the network and it's catching on like wildfire. This product is so simplistic and yet so effective. Who would have thought a cobblestone street for pedestrians and docile bicyclist with high-end designer shops and upscale specialty merchants would be so popular?"

At that moment Uli took his hands off his knees and slowly eased his body backward until his back rested deep within the auburn leather chair. His chest stuck out, his elbows rest comfortably on the armrest of the chair. His height fell six inches short of the top of the chair's high backrest. He was in a daze, soaking in the praise.

Opa's voice began to register once again.

"Its name, The King's Alley, adds a lot of prestige to the concept. When someone is seen shopping here, they know two things for sure: it's top quality and it's expensive. I also like the touch that the flower shop along with the fish market and butcher will bring. It really reminds me and others who have European roots of home." Opa didn't reveal it but he expected to fill the two small shops with small businesses connected to the charity shelter in North Jacksonville. He would invite them personally and assist with relocation, if he must.

"Thank you, sir." Uli belted with pride.

A mature woman in unbelievable shape walked in with tea and coffee on a tray. The once-blond beauty, now adorned with shining gray tresses pinned up in a bun, smiled as she poured Opa's cup of black coffee and walked off. Mrs. Davis is the only secretary Opa ever had. He took a sip and stayed focused. "We have plans to put a King's Alley on the north side of Jacksonville. There is somewhat of a mall there now but our team feels that an upscale product will do well for the area by pulling in the locals." He sipped the coffee again, and Uli sat quietly.

"The Amelia Island community and surrounding beaches along with the southern Georgia market are our target clients. I want you to spearhead this project and I wanted to personally tell you of our plans."

"It would be an honor, sir."

Opa took a long drag of the coffee, then a deep breath.

"So how was the business trip?" He asked to Uli's surprise.

"It was fine. I did a lot of networking for the company and acquired a few new ideas for Star."

"My granddaughter was so disappointed she couldn't join you."

"Yes. I know. There was so much to do and not enough personal time for her and me. She would have been miserable and I didn't want to put her through that. We worked diligently establishing a new network and setting up the infrastructure. So when I returned to my hotel room, I was done. Our mornings started really early."

Opa didn't respond, instead he poured another cup of coffee.

"As a matter of fact, I am meeting your granddaughter in a few minutes, she and Roger are picking me up for lunch."

Mrs. Davis voice came over the intercom. "Mr. Lang, Dr. Ava is here."

"Thank you, send her in."

"Opa, how are you?" Ava greeted him with a hug and a kiss. The greeting between she and Uli was rudimentary at best with a peck on his cheek and no affection from him. "Are you ready, Uli?"

"Yes. Let me get my jacket."

In the car, not one word was spoken on the way to the restaurant. Uli got out of the car and held the door for her.

"Thank you," she said.

He opened the door to the restaurant.

"Thank you."

He pulled her chair.

"Thank you, again."

The waiter took their drink order and left.

"What you just did on our way from the car, I love that. I need that. I love to have my doors opened. I love for my chair to be pulled, and I love time with my husband. But I don't want to have to go to his job after being disappointed two weeks to make that happen." She looked into his eyes. His glance was different. "We used to love so well before," she said.

Uli nodded.

"Let's start dating again. I know we are married and have been for some time now, but I still love to be courted. The same things you did to get me, I need some of that to sustain me."

"I know. I hear what you're saying. It just wasn't the right time or situation during that trip to Europe. When I found out how demanding it was going be, I didn't want to put you through that and I should have considered that early on before inviting you."

"Did you ever think about letting me make my own decision? That I might know what was too demanding for me or what was not enough time together. Enough for me would have cost you nothing. When you were finished with your day, just coming to our room and cuddling, then letting me fall asleep next to you, that would have been enough for me."

"I didn't know," he admitted. "I should have let you decide. Honestly, I get it," he said with finality. She knew from his tone that he had not considered a word she was saying.

"I've been so focused on Star Real Estate and my position. I know you understand that, Ava. And now I have my chance. Your grandfather has a new project that he wants me to oversee. He was truly impressed with the preparation of our King's Alley. He said it was a great job. And my business partners have a few more loose ends to tie up here and overseas, and then I am all yours. We can start on the baby making full steam ahead."

She leaned over to the right and kissed him softly on the lips. "Honey, let me talk to Opa. He's all about family. He will take care of everything and give you time. And your business partners, can't they wait, too? We are not strapped for money or anything else. I am sure they need you more than you need them."

"I can't do that. People are counting on me. Our future is counting on this."

"I see," she said and glanced over his shoulder outside the window to keep her eyes from revealing her hurt. "You don't understand. And I am not happy with that."

"Ava, don't be mad."

"I'm not mad. I'm just telling you what I need. And you told me what you are willing to give. I understand clearly."

They ate their lunch in silence.

Roger dropped Ava off at the hospital and returned Uli to the office. Once back in his office, Uli confirmed the night's final late meeting and convinced himself that he could direct all of his evenings around her schedule as soon as he came home tomorrow morning.

CHAPTER EIGHTEEN

~~~~~~

Ten forty-five p.m. and his last meeting was about to take place. The two business partners walked into the small office completely rattled. The man with the long scar said, "We might have to lay low for a while because there is talk about people going to the U.S. authorities. I don't want to be locked up again."

Uli stared at him, then finally said, "Think about it. I am a respected V. P. of the largest real estate development firm in the entire state of Florida. Who in their right mind would believe their accusations? Besides, I don't think they have the nerve to go to the authorities knowing I have hundreds of lawyers at my disposal. You goons think you're smart, so tell me how do you think this sounds?" Uli changed his voice to sound like a squeaky woman, "I donated a kidney to come to the United States. I donated a liver so my family could be smuggled into America, and Mr. Kärcher reneged on his word and is holding my passport.'"

He changed to his normal voice with a huff, "Remember this is not the first time these people have threaten this. If they come forward, what do they have? Nothing! And then they will be sent back to the hell they were in before I gave them a better life working for me and building my town centers. They should just be glad they are better off now than they were before!"

The two goons rescinded into their seats and offered no defense.

"I know I am right," Uli said, leaning back in his chair and kicking his feet on top of the oak desk. "What we really need to be concentrating on is my latest venture. It makes revenue from these construction projects look like peanuts." He gave a broad, ominous smile. "We are getting thirty times the profit of any business I have ever been involved in. The beauty about that is I don't see an end in sight."

CHAPTER NINETEEN

~~~~~~

Calvin walked into A1A with anticipation. He couldn't remember the last time butterflies were in his stomach in hopes of someone's presence. He wondered if she would be there again.

The thought was quickly answered when the first person he spotted was Ava wearing a sleeveless, peach-colored dress that laid gently across her slim, muscular frame.

"Hello, stranger. I see you're showing off those Michelle Obama arms of yours."

"A girls got to do what a girls got do," She said jokingly.

"I remember the little strength exhibition you displayed at the terminal. You are pretty strong."

"That was pure adrenaline. When a life is at stake, you'll be surprise at what you can do."

Calvin looked at the chair beside her and saw the stack of reading material. She was back at it again: eating alone, studying, and looking gorgeous. He thought back to the days with Déjà.

"Studying?"

"More like researching." She held up two medical books. But

Calvin's attention was on the small book remaining in the chair. "What's that magazine?"

"Info on the new sensation of shopping malls here in Jacksonville," she said a little boastfully. "The King's Alley."

"No the other one."

"Oh that's an equipment catalog by Leo Jordan. Best gym equipment money can buy. But the waiting list is two years out."

"Two years?"

"Yes. But trust me it is worth the wait. Sometimes you have to wait for things that are worthwhile."

Calvin smiled as Déjà's spirit showed up again. She often said those exact words. "Calvin, would you please sit," she wasn't asking.

He pulled back the chair and beckoned for the waiter. "Hey, Kent, how's it going, man?" They shook hands. "Working smart, Mr. C. Working smart."

"Stay at it, Youngblood. We need you around," Calvin said quickly.

"I'll get your water right out to you. Do you want anything else right now? I think you might like the seared tuna with a lil' extra wasabi." Kent gestured towards Ava's dish.

"That'll work for me. Thanks," Calvin said. He noticed Ava's empty plate. "I guess I'll be eating alone."

She chuckled.

"I just had this epiphany," Ava said. "This really is your favorite restaurant! I frequent this place when I need to be in a different world."

She played with a thought several times until the anxiety built, warming her body. "What do say we plan to join one another here when you see me and I'm alone—that's if you are not on a date or having a dinner meeting."

She took a deep swallow of air.

"I'd like that, Ava. Your company is rewarding." She smiled and with newfound bravery she released her next opinion. "Maybe I could even convince you to think about slowly dating." To his own surprise, no instant rebuttal shot from his lips.

As they ate, laughed, and debated Jacksonville politics, Calvin began thinking he was already on a date—and he wasn't sure if dating was safe for him, especially when he can notice Déjà sitting across the room in the corner, relaxed, and waiting for him.

CHAPTER TWENTY

~~~~~~

The next morning after he finished his routine, Calvin decided to take the day off. He walked around the house in his black polo bottom pajamas with no shirt, doing busy work when he could feel Déjà enter the room. *How are you, Baby?"* Her voice was so clear, so serene; it amazed him.

Calvin answered, "I'm fine, Love," with a slight tone of guilt.

Why the tone?

Calvin hesitated then answered, "You were with me last night. I saw you in the corner. I heard your voice at the table and I smelled your scent."

Tell me about her.

"I'm committed to you," his voice revealed the confusion bubbling inside of him.

Yes, you were very committed to me, but we are not-"

He interrupted her, not wanting to hear her say they were no longer together. "She's so much like you. She's strong and smart like you. She has this unorthodox sense of humor. Her laugh. Her figure. Her mind. She smells like you. She talks like you," he shook his head and walked aimlessly around the room, careful not to bump into anything.

"Déjà, did you manifest this? Is this your doing, Déjà? If so, it's pretty cruel."

Calvin, you are with the living. You have to move on. You deserve to be loved. You deserve to be able to love someone else. I am only here because you won't let me go. She is a lot like me so let her friendship help you and maybe her love can keep you.

Calvin shook his head reluctantly as her words repeated in his mind and rippled through his heart.

Do me a favor and call my brother. He will tell you the same thing. If she is a good woman and wants to love you and give you lots of babies, you have my blessing. There should be a lot of little Calvin's for the young ladies coming up. But, Baby, I have to go.

He sat on the couch, mesmerized by what had just happened and fearful that Déjà was now permanently gone. For little longer than an hour, he sat still and allowed his soul to cry.

Then, he called Leo.

"Leo. What's up boy?"

"Calvin! Man, it's great to hear your voice."

"It's great hearing yours, too."

"Man! I miss talking to you. Things really changed after my sister passed."

Calvin agreed. "Yes, it did. Do you have some time to fly to the east coast?"

"For you, my brother, I will make time. What's up?"

Calvin paused for a moment. "I have a friend that is serious about her gym and she is two years out on your list. She has no idea you're my brother-in-law."

"Hold on and let me grab my tablet to check my schedule." Leo's phone went silent.

"I'm back, Bro. What about three months from today?"

"That will be great. I don't know how to thank you."

"Oh, yes, you do! Jenkins Barbecue, here we come!"

"It's a deal! See you in three months. I love you, Bro."

The next phone call Calvin made was to Cheryl. Her phone barely rang once when she answered, "Hey, Cal."

"Sis. What's up?"

"Nothing. What's up with you?"

"I think it's time we get momma out the 'hood. I think we need to find a nice, plush place where she can attract upscale clientele. Can you do some real estate research and let me know how we can secure something?"

Cheryl didn't hesitate with her answer. "I was thinking the same thing when I last visited the store."

"So you know, then" Calvin said. "With this new Bird of Paradise flower commitment she has, the current location can remain the warehouse and community store, but she really needs that expansion. Besides, she deserves it."

Cheryl agreed. "The research has already been done. The best place I found that would allow for the type of return on investment that she would need would be the new town center development that they are calling King's Alley. They have storefront vacancies, and the renter's contract for certified minority businesses is one of the fairest I've seen in a long time. Mom's 8-a certification qualifies her to even become a subcontractor for the developers if the opportunity ever presents itself."

Calvin thought about it as Cheryl briefed him. "But there are other developments in process and you can get in at bidding level and open on day one with this same real estate group."

After assessing all the info Cheryl offered, he told her, "Now is the time for momma not to worry about a thing. I would love for her to find a place where she can relax while doing her thing and still make money. If you ask me, Sis, the King's Alley Town Center is that place. Get the contracts and floor plans and whatever other information we need and let's try to make it happen, ASAP," he said.

Cheryl could tell he was smiling. His voice always changed when he gave a big smile. It had been a long time since she heard him smile, and she loved it.

"Thanks, Sis, for everything," he said before hanging up. Calvin stood in front of the mirror, as he got dressed for dinner at A1A. Being a little silly, he made goo goo eyes at his reflection.

"Man, I really hope Ava will be there tonight. If I bump into her that will keep the streak going. I would have seen her at least once every week since meeting her four months ago. Now that's a good thing," he said.

~~~~~~

Calvin climbed those stairs so many times before but this particular night his heart pounded like it was trying to come out of his chest. When he made it to the top and saw Ava sitting in his favorite spot, a smile ran through his entire body.

"You made it," he said as he slid into the seat. "I must say, you look lovely, young lady." Ava blushed. "Thank you, Calvin. You look dashing, also."

"I'm leaving town for ten days. It's a surgeon's conference where I will be presenting on pediatric robotic surgery," she said following one quick breath.

Calvin knew the surgery well. For many nights, he watched and listened to Déjà studying the same topic. She had a heart for children. The thought of Déjà wanting to conceive before she left on assignment brought him a brief moment of sadness as he looked at

Ava who was glowing with excitement.

"This is something close to my heart because I love children!" Calvin could do nothing but smile as those words rolled off her tongue.

"Maybe we can video chat once or twice so you can keep me up on the things happening in exciting Jacksonville. I may need your energy and smile to get me through these grueling meetings," she joked.

"I'll hold you to that," he said.

CHAPTER TWENTY-ONE

~~~~~~

At 9 a.m, an 18-wheeler followed by a customized van pulled up in front of the gym. Painted on the two-vehicle convoy was a gigantic picture of famed football player and exercise physiologist Leo Jordan. Five workers wearing red, tailor-made jumpers got out the van and headed to the entrance.

That's strange, Ava thought. By her calculations, Schwarz was still twenty-one months out on the waiting list. It was confirmed in the last correspondence she received from the company.

She saw a shiny, black 500SL AMG Mercedes, pull up directly behind the van. To her surprise, the next person she saw was Leo Jordan.

Her shock kept her from noticing the workers walking through the gym, looking at the walls and ceiling, unplugging equipment, and checking mirrors. Once he entered the building, the workers walked over towards him but he talked with Ava first.

"Calvin Hollaway told me you needed my help but you were two years out. A friend of his is a friend of mine." Leo extended his hand.

"I'm Ava Kärcher." She shook his hand.

"Pleased to meet you, Dr. Kärcher."

A female worker gave him a clipboard and signaled for the crew to get started. She gave Ava a smile and said, "Ladies-only, huh?" Ava shook her head and the two women gave each other a knowing smile. "We'll get started," she said to Leo. He nodded.

"So how do you know Calvin?"

"We played football together at The University of Miami. Calvin could have played in the NFL. But the call to protect freedom was much too loud to ignore for him."

"Calvin also persuaded me to join the military with him. I am glad I served. It helped me in many ways. I owe my business and my success to all the gym owners—like you—who opened shop for me to train during my time in the military. It's how and where my empire was born," Leo shared. "Calvin was with me every step of the way."

Ava was amazed. *Calvin is wonderful. I can't lose him. I need his support and friendship right now.* She told herself.

Ava checked her letter and it was just as she thought. "Mr. Jordan, I am two years out on the list," she said offering him the letter.

"That letter is void. My team is here today to install your equipment and transform this place into a Leo Jordan training site. And, we won't leave until we have it to specifications. You have my word on it."

"Thank you so much, Mr. Jordan."

"Don't worry about a thing. My crew and I have everything under control."

Ava smiled and said, "My manager, Sheila, will answer any question you may have. She's standing near the classroom over there," Ava pointed. "I need to get back to the hospital."

Ava grabbed her satchel from behind the counter, waved to Sheila, and left.

Before getting out of her car and going into Mayo, Ava closed her eyes and whispered, "Father God, I thank you for Calvin."

When she opened her eyes, she saw a bright orange van from Hollaway's Haven drive pass her vehicle heading toward the hospital's entrance. A beautiful painting of three bouquets of stargazers, Gerber daisies, and Bird of Paradise flowers wrapped the sides of the vehicle.

She made a phone call. "Good morning, Mr. Hollaway. I see you are full of surprises." She heard him smile before he spoke. "I take it Leo has paid you a visit."

"Yes, he has, and I will deal with you when I see you tonight at dinner, if you have time." Calvin laughed.

"I will make the time." He heard her laugh. "Why thank you, sir," she said. "I have to go in now. See you tonight."

~~~~~~

Calvin pulled up to Jenkins Barbecue and parked to the left of Leo who was already parked. The two got out and hugged.

"Man! It's been too long, Calvin."

"You're right, Leo."

"I know my sister is no longer with us. But you know I love you like my own brother."

Calvin placed his hand on Leo's shoulder. "I know. Let's go inside, Bruh."

Leo smiled as he said, "You know just how to bribe a brother, don't you? I would never turn down great barbecue."

As soon as they were served, Leo broke the ice, "My sister would approve of her," he said, lifting a juicy baby back rib to his mouth. His fingertips were covered with the best honey barbecue sauce he had ever tasted. A staunch healthy eater, Leo allowed himself to indulge in Jenkins' sweet, mild sauce, baked beans, potato salad, two slices of pecan pie, and a large sweet tea. The extra lemon was probably the healthiest thing in his meal.

"Listen, Calvin," Leo said in a serious tone. "Déjà would have never wanted you to become a monk. My sister would want you to go on living your life with someone. She would just hope the woman treated you right and loved you as much as she did. This I know."

Tears filled Calvin's eyes.

"Thank you so much, Leo, for saying that. I know just how close you and your sister were. I just wouldn't think of talking to another woman without getting the opinion of the only person in the world who knew her as well as I did."

"So, where did you meet her?"

With a slight chuckle Calvin said, "The cruise terminal."

"What? I can't Mr. No-Way-in-Hell-Would-I-Ever-Date-a-Woman-from-Party-Ships!"

"Wait. She was not on a cruise; she was picking up some people when a passenger had a heart attack and she sprung into action."

"I must say she is sexy in scrubs and the white coat looks good, too. But I never would let her know what I was thinking."

Calvin explained the day he first saw Ava and the circumstances of their first dinner together. He didn't have to work hard to persuade Leo on how different Ava was and how much she was like Déjà. He also told Leo about the missing heirloom.

After sucking the barbecue off of all ten fingers, Leo saw the look on Calvin's face and said. "You have it bad, my brother."

"No, I don't."

Then after a few seconds, Calvin admitted. "Okay, I guess I do." He hesitated before continuing, "I know this may be hard to believe but she reminds me so much of Déjà. We talk a few times during the day about things that truly matter. I love the way she speaks. I love the tone of her voice. I love the way she walks. I love the way she tilts her head, the way she moves her hands."

"Listen to what you just said! You sound like a love puppy."

"Yeah. I do, don't I?"

"Yes. You do." They both laughed.

~~~~~~

Leo kept his word and everything was exactly to Ava's specifications. When the crew let her in to see the final setup, she was thrilled. New ab machines, black and pink spin bikes, foot gear, gloves, hydration rakes, yoga blocks, and dumbbells. Even the locker room was redesigned to look like the entrance to a spa. Small towers of Leo Jordan stainless steel water bottles sat discreetly in the corners throughout the building. His women's multi-vitamins and energy drink mix were on sale behind the new counters. Leo Jordan's female worker handed her a box of gym shirts embroidered with the Schwarz logo and "a Leo Jordan certified site" etched beneath it.

"This is for your team," she said. "Welcome to our team." She gave Ava a wink.

Ava looked at the final bill and said, "You made a mistake in the billing. This price is thirty percent less than what was on the contract."

"That price doesn't have the family discount on it," Leo said as he ripped up the old contract.

"I can't accept that."

"What kind of friend would I be? I have known Calvin a long time. It would hurt my pride if I couldn't do this for him. Take this as a gift of the friendship between him and me. Please."

"Thank you, Leo. You and Calvin are such sweethearts." Ava gave him a light kiss on the cheek.

"You're welcome. Take care of Calvin."

"I will. I promise."

Sheila walked through the gym, taking photographs and calling Schwarz members to come by for an impromptu celebration. Ava called Calvin as soon as Leo and his team pulled off. "I was wondering if you would like to have dinner with me tonight?"

"I can't think of anything more I would rather do than have dinner with you, Lady."

"I would love to come and pick you up from your home as any respectable man would. But I am not going to push. In time, you will tell me when you are ready for that. But if you don't mind, please meet me in St. Augustine at A1A Ale Works."

"I don't mind. As a matter of fact, I would love to."

For this dinner, Ava put extra effort into her appearance. The dress, the heels, and the hair all subtly screamed sexy. She even added a little extra Love in White around her ear and above her breast. Oma appeared as Ava did her final look over in the mirror.

Ava. You need to slow this down. This man. He is not your husband.

Ava paused for a slight second looking throughout the room to see Oma who stood in front of the open window. Oma stepped to the side away from the light so she could be seen against the tan walls. "Oma," Ava said softly. She wanted so desperately to tell her every detail of the emotions she was feeling towards Calvin and how it clashed with those she had for Uli. Instead she said, "Oma, this is harmless."

Child, look at the way you're dressed. This is not your husband! Oma said with a little more emotion.

"Oh, Oma. I know this isn't my husband. This man did something to help me without looking for anything."

He will want something in return, Ava. You are not a naïve woman.

"Oma, there's no quid pro quo." Every time we see each other, he has been nothing less than a gentleman. As a matter of fact, you are right, Oma, he is not my husband. He is the only man who is not my blood relative that went out and did something for me. I didn't have to ask. That is something your husband, my Opa, would do for you. My husband doesn't. But my friend does."

Oma made her final attempt to extinguish the flames she felt brewing between her granddaughter and the beautiful Black man who resembled a special friend of Oma's from decades ago. *Back up, child, focus on your surgeries, your home, and the gym. Focus on having a family.* Oma's spirit faded away.

Ava walked out the door.

~~~~~~

At 8:20 p.m., Ava entered A1A. Calvin was already seated when the maitre d' escorted her to the table. Calvin stood up and went to her side of the table and pulled her chair for her. "Thank you, Alex," he told the maitre d'. By the time he made it back to his chair, he was rewarded with the biggest smile he'd ever seen from Ava.

"I want to say thanks for what you did. You didn't have to, and I am grateful." Calvin returned the smile.

"Calvin, I love the fact that we have conveniently bumped into one another almost weekly. It has been a pure joy." Ava said as she placed her napkin in her lap. "By no means am I complaining or probing but may I ask you something? I am curious."

Calvin took his napkin off the table and placed it in his lap.

"Why did you ask the favor of Leo?"

"I simply believe in supporting hard workers, beautiful people, and honest friends. You are all of the above."

"That's a heck of a gesture, Calvin. Honestly, it's so much more than a friend would do."

Calvin flashed another smile. "It's just how I am wired. Giving makes me happy."

Ava paused for a second.

"You must come by and look at the fabulous job Leo's team did."

Calvin nodded in agreement while he felt a little soreness in his cheeks from all the smiling he had done over the last six months.

"Tell me, Calvin, what's your biggest dream? What's your Hollaway legacy?"

"If we're talking short term, it would mean the world to me to be able to do something special that I've been working on for my mother. I would love to open a second flower shop for her. She deserves one in a luxury location. I would love for this one to be a high-end store, a place where she could work without the grunge. Her employees and I could grind at the greenhouse, but I want my mother to be the investor who shows up because she loves it, not because she has to."

Ava listened intensely; when he finished she gave her real estate advice. "I see two possibilities. One would be The Town Center. The other would be a new concept called The Kings Alley. The Town Center is the more established one but both fit the bill. I suggest you send in bids to them both." She envisioned the possibility of them having a special project together, and then said, "We can do this!"

When those words rolled off her tongue, Calvin instinctively put his right hand in the air. Ava slapped his hand and laughed. The only thing missing was the kiss after the high-five that Déjà always delivered. This took his breath away.

"Ava, I'll be back."

"Is everything alright, Calvin?"

"Sure. I just need to use the little boy's room."

Oma appeared at the table. *I told you to slow down, Ava. This is dangerous. This is not your husband. And now you are working to build this man's dreams. Slow. Down. Ava.*

"You made my point exactly, Oma. It is dangerous. It is extremely dangerous to have a husband who doesn't love you and doesn't support you. It is not dangerous to have a friend, Oma. I deserve a man who is this thoughtful and caring. I work hard in everything I do, like a good German girl. I deserve to have Calvin in my life."

Two tears raced down her face. Calvin saw the tears as he walked up and asked, "Ava, what's wrong? Why are you crying?"

"Sorry, Calvin. I am just happy for you and about everything that has happened today and these last couple of months."

CHAPTER TWENTY-TWO

~~~~~~

Uli had quite a bit to do in Jacksonville. When his workload was this heavy, he preferred to work close to home. His first choice was always the upscale neighborhood location, a four-minute drive away from the house.

He worked up until the wee hours of the morning, hoping this crop was as good as his two partners claimed it to be. He would have to make time in the near future to fly to Europe before delivery.

Uli devised a plan that was only meaningful to him. This allowed the ability to work on his projects no matter who walked in and interrupted. Even if Ava walked in, which was highly unlikely, she would not be able to decipher his system. Uli created a handwritten ledger based on his passion: classical music. He separated his clients into categories named after his favorite composers, starting with Bach.

Johann Sebastian Bach was a member of the baroque era, known for his extravagantly expressing style of music. This category was reserved for his top-end clients who had no financial restraints. Lik Bach, these clients were the first choice.

Uli's Wolfgang Amadeus Mozart category held the names of clientele who were more the middle of the pack. They sought companionship and impressive eye candy.

The Ludwig Van Beethoven category named all clients seeking the entire package. They were the ones who were always looking for attraction, companionship, domestic skills, and even marriage.

Richard Wagner was added as a category for two reasons: the connection to his Dresden roots, and since he was into opera and theatre, this made Wagner one of Uli's favorites. These females must be an attraction and able to sing or perform. That was the calling card of clients in this category.

While he completed the work in his ledger, his two goons walked into the office. Uli gestured towards the two seats in front of his desk, "sit." He then asked the question burning in his gut. "Tell me about this crop. How good is it? Really."

"Uli we're not telling you something we've been told. We just flew back and saw them with our own eyes. It's 3 a.m. and the first place we came is to your office. That alone should tell you that this is something you need to see for yourself."

"I must admit. I have been hearing a lot of good things about this crop. So are you sure this is that much of a top-of-the-line crop? I really need to be sure because I have found the perfect clients and I want to make a tremendous impression on them."

The man with the long scar removed his black hat and placed it on his knee and spoke. "Boss, we have seen it. We know you only have one chance to make a first impression and if we blow it, we blow it for you. That could make you the biggest joke in the business. All we are asking is for you to check it out yourself. You won't be disappointed. We're going to be set for life and that is no exaggeration."

After finishing the shot glass of tequila, Uli reached to the bottom and took out the worm, slowly placed it in his mouth, and chewed slowly. He looked over at the other guy as he asked, "You both feel that way?"

"Yes." They said in unison.

"I have a new way to introduce the product to the high-end clients to ensure they get the most bang for their buck. Right off the top, they will get the best we have to offer. As a matter of fact, I want to fly into Europe and hand-select this crop. There is a certain dollar amount that I want to demand and if we don't have a top-end product, we will be just like those other riffraff. I am not willing to risk going to jail for scraps. I will start the ball rolling tomorrow."

He decided he would tell Opa that he needed to fly back to Germany for research. He knew Opa would not care how long he would be gone once he realized Germany was the destination.

Uli looked at the clock on the wall and ended the meeting abruptly. He'd promised Ava he'd stop meeting all night.

~~~~~~

The next morning, Ava heard Uli making his way to the breakfast table to join her.

"Guten Morgen, Ava." Uli spoke before he joined her.

She gave no reply.

Ava was locked in a daydream of Calvin, her renovated gym, and Calvin's new flower shop. She stared at her phone, admiring the photos Sheila sent of new members enjoying the new Leo Jordan equipment. The new check-in counter with her golden logo beamed the most light in the photo and brightened her smile.

"Guten Morgen." This time, he spoke louder. His voice registered and she replied with a bright smile. "Oh, I'm sorry, Uli. Guten Morgen." She placed her phone on the table face up when Uli came over to kiss her cheek. He glanced at the phone and noticed the new gym equipment. He shrugged it off as unimportant and took his seat at the table. "How did you sleep?"

"I slept well. How did it go at the office?"

"Same as usual. Grinding and working every hour that I can. I will be going to Europe in a couple of days, and, you—."

"I hope you have a productive trip," she said quickly before he could offer for her to join him.

"Well, what does your schedule look like?" He asked with a concerned look.

"Uli, I really don't want to crowd you. Promise me you'll be careful and don't work too hard. Make sure you get some sleep after your meetings. Please?"

With a confused look, his mouth stayed partially opened. He didn't know if he should feel relieved that she wasn't going or concerned that she absolutely didn't seem to care one way or another. After he made several attempts to make small talk, he asked, "Are you going to be fine?"

"Oh, yes. I just don't want you to overwork yourself. I believe you are doing this for the future, and I love you for that."

"Okay," he replied.

Ava tried to control her excitement.

The once-a-week romantic rendezvous in St. Augustine, having dinner, and talking until 10 p.m. could now be extended. Time with Calvin was always intoxicating and a short two-hour stint was never enough. She considered inviting Calvin to the house or suggesting that she could meet at his home. She never knew what time Uli would return home from the office but he never returned before eleven. Disrespecting Uli was not an option, but Ava had done everything her grandparents asked of her. Oma gave the template for how to be the perfect wife. From teaching her to "sit and not be seen" to "let the husband order the meal," Ava had followed every rule and every piece of advice Oma or her spirit had given to Ava over the years. This was the first time that Ava questioned that style of marriage for her day and time.

When Ava showed up for dinner, Calvin stood up as she approached the table. He kissed her softly on the cheek as she handed him a wrapped gift. "What is this?"

"It's a CD. Marvin Gaye and his greatest hits." Calvin smiled as he unwrapped his gift. He smiled and stared at the CD. "Thank you so much I am going to enjoy this immensely."

That evening while the two were having dinner, Calvin took a quick glance at his watch and said, "I know it's getting near the time you have to leave. So, will I see you next week?"

"Go ahead. Let's finish our conversation. Opa isn't going to miss me. I have time."

"Are you sure?"

"I am sure. I have time for anything. I am feeling more comfortable with you." Ava took a small sip of wine and looked into Calvin's eyes as if she were a young student with a crush on her professor.

"Comfortable enough to take a late-night carriage ride to the fort and around the city?"

"Yes," she replied with starry eyes.

After getting in the carriage, Calvin placed his arm around her and she nuzzled in the space he provided just under his arm.

"I really don't want to be at home right now. It's just going to make me think about my Opa. He's ninety years old. He is my last living relative. No one else can reach back into our family past. I lost my Oma, a year ago. She taught me so much when I lost my parents. Opa and Roger are in New York putting flowers on my Oma's grave. It had to be destiny for those two. Their mothers were great friends and they all grew up together." Feeling herself rambling, she stopped the flow of that conversation and moved on. "Thank you so much for this time, Calvin. I'm in no hurry to get to that empty house."

"No problem. I am here for you, Ava. That, you can be sure of. I have time."

They rode around for about another hour when she looked at her watch. "Dang! It's already past one. I am sorry. I know you have to work later today." Calvin watched her talk and smiled slowly.

"Honestly, I must admit I've never had a better date in my life than this one," she confessed. "If I did, I certainly can't remember when."

"I am having a great time, too, Ava. If you want to stay, we can keep on riding."

"You are so sweet, but you won't be worth anything at work if you don't head home now."

Calvin walked her to the car. "I am parked a little ways back but do me a favor, please. Wait for me so I can follow you and make sure you get safely on I-95. I'll follow until you get to your exit. If you don't mind, call me when you get inside your home so I'll know you made it in okay."

Wow. What a gentleman. I deserve this. Ava thought. She made it on to the interstate with Calvin in tow. Just before they entered into Duval County, her cell rang. She allowed the Bluetooth to register and connect the call, "Hey!" She said.

"Get off here. Get off at this exit. Then, follow me."

She obeyed.

Calvin pulled into the Phantom Fireworks parking lot.

"Let's Get It On" by Marvin Gaye was blasting from his Tesla's speakers. "This is my favorite song. May I have this dance?" Ava nodded. He grabbed her in his arms. She felt his power and still felt safe as he held her close. *Yes. This couldn't be any better.* They both thought. Ava allowed herself to enjoy the sexy, caring man who held her and the great music as they slow danced under the stars and moonlight. No question this was the best date ever.

CHAPTER TWENTY-THREE

~~~~~~

The next morning Ava was still a little tired when she arrived at the gym. But she had to share the good news about Dr. Abou Diallo.

"Sheila, I am so happy to tell you that Abou, the guy from the cruise who had the heart attack, has been released from therapy. He has made it home safely and is healed."

"Delivery. Delivery for Ava Kärcher."

Sheila grabbed the two colossal arrangements of Birds of Paradise stemming from two oblong, glass vases, as Ava tipped the delivery guy.

"Those are beautiful flowers! That African family has great taste. Do you think they came from Africa?"

"No," Ava chuckled.

"What kind are they?"

"Those are Birds of Paradise, which just happen to be my favorite." *He listened. How thoughtful is that?* Ava thought. Sheila found a card. Ava held her breath as Sheila read the card aloud. She hoped that Calvin could be discrete. "The card says, 'Thanks for being beautiful. I hope you enjoy."

Ava breathed a sigh of relief. Calvin walked in to everyone's surprise. "Mr. Hollaway." Ava extended her hand to Calvin. He followed her lead without skipping a beat.

"You're the longshoreman from the cruise terminal." Sheila noticed. "Man, this is a great day! First, the guy who had the heart attack is released and now a visit from you." Calvin took that information as an opening.

"So, Mr. Abou is doing better?"

"Yes, sir. He is doing much better."

"I am glad to hear that."

Sheila interrupted once again. "So where do you work out? Hollaway is your name, right?" Calvin stood in one spot as he looked around. "Yes. Calvin Hollaway."

"We are not coed. But I would be honored to give you a tour. As a matter of fact, we just finished renovations and we are proud of the setup. So, if you know any ladies looking for a gym, please tell them about us."

After the tour, Sheila walked into the office wearing latex gloves and cleaning supplies to clean off an area to put the flowers. Calvin grabbed a pair of gloves to help. He tried to pass Ava a pair. A look of sheer terror took over her face in an instant.

"I have a severe case of sensitivity to latex. One touch could send me into anaphylactic shock, which could be fatal."

"I had no idea."

"No problem. There's no way you could have known."

"I have to get to work. I hope you enjoy the flowers."

"Oh, I will. Let me walk you to your car."

This guy has to be too good to be true.

When she walked him to the car, he planted the softest kiss she'd ever felt in her life on her cheek. She stood there frozen. Then, she walked back in the gym in a trance.

She was getting in over her head and fast. Everything was fine until he touched her. That changed everything. She lost control from that moment on, and the worst part was she knew it.

Why did Opa have to leave while Uli was away? Why didn't I just go with them to New York? I gave Calvin this "Til Death Do Us Part" spill. How hypocritical is that? My grandparents had a few storms and my Oma told me men folks are men folks. I know what I must do. I will end it this evening at dinner. I know I am over my head. I need to stop it now.

Her cell phone rang.

"Hi, Ava."

"Hello, Calvin."

"I know we've seen each other every evening this week but I am so wondering if you could make time for me tonight?"

"Of course, I can. I need to see you, too."

They made plans. "I'd like to surprise you. Don't go into A1A when you arrive. Just wait for me outside, so we can go in together."

~~~~~~

Ava arrived at 7:30 p.m. planning to wait thirty minutes for his arrival. To her surprise, Calvin was already waiting. "What time did you get here?"

"I can't tell you that," he joked. "You see when I was in the military the rule was 'if you are there at the precise time, that means you are already late.'"

She smiled and nodded. "So, shall we go up stairs?"

"We aren't going in."

"Huh?"

"But we are having dinner. Come with me." She gladly walked

with him, wondering what type of surprise he had planned. One thing she learned in the few months of knowing Calvin was that she had better brace herself and hold on to her panties. A surprise from him normally packed two fierce punches: romanticism and heart-tugging emotion. She was still reeling from the dance underneath the stars. That was a clear T.K.O. She knew if he'd thrown one more punch, it was over for her, and she knew she shouldn't be thinking that way.

They stopped in front of Casa de Sueños Inn, a beautiful mini-castle. "This is our destination."

"A bed and breakfast?"

"Yes."

When they walked in, the main dinning table was set for two. The scent of a burnt match still lingered. Calvin led her to the small table and pulled out her chair. He walked away, leaving her anxiously waiting. He returned to the table with a pan of Paella de Marisco.

"Who cooked this?"

"I did. This is special Paella made with fish, shellfish, and chicken. I see how health-conscious you are, so I made certain that tonight you don't have to worry about a thing. Normally this Paella is accompanied with rice but we're going to have noodles." He poured her a glass of Robert Mondavi's Cabernet Sauvignon. And for him a glass of the coldest water he could stand. "I've been working on this meal all day, immediately after they closed the kitchen for breakfast this morning."

"How did you set this up?"

"I will never tell." He sat next to her and began feeding her bits of shrimp with his hands while gazing into her eyes. "The dish you're eating originated in the fields of Valencia, Spain. So I felt it only fitting to rent the Valencia room. It's on the second floor. It's really a romantic escape with plush texture and a Hemmingway theme. But if you choose not to stay tonight it's perfectly fine, too. I hope the meal is enjoyable enough for you."

Damn. So much for the being strong and ending this. Ava thought.

"Am I being too forward?" He asked, noticing a shift in her disposition.

"No, not at all."

After dinner, he took her by the hand and they walked up the stairs. "Wait here for a moment."

"Another surprise?"

"No, Ava. This is a gift. It's all a gift for you," he said opening the door. "Okay. You can come in."

When she walked in, Calvin handed her a Victoria Secret bag with pink tissue wrapping hiding the gift. He pointed to the restroom and said, "I took the liberty of getting you something. I hope you like it. Go see."

To her surprise she found nothing tight, nothing pushed up, and nothing to squeeze into. He'd bought her a conservative, silk camisole with matching pants. She gave the outfit a smile. *I am perfectly fine with this.* Here she was with the body she had worked so hard to keep, and he wanted her to completely cover it up. *That's sweet and classy. What a true gentleman. Who said chivalry is dead?*

When she returned to the bedroom, he gently laid her body on the bed and kissed her on the lips for the first time.

What a kisser! His lips are soft as hospital cotton. Ava became lost in the kiss. The next thing she knew, he straddled her and patted her down like a police officer. But she didn't make one complaint. Truth be told she was too focused on his chest when he took off his shirt. With nothing but his silk pants on, she stared at his massive pectorals as they hung. Unable to resist any longer she touched one. *Man, that's hard!*

When the two interlocked fingers, he placed her hands over her head. He stopped his lips less than an inch from hers. His minty-fresh breath was so intoxicating. He whispered, "Are you okay?" Speechless, she nodded then felt a kiss softer than the first. His tongue gently touched her lips and waited until hers lips parted giving his tongue permission to enter. Then, his tongue greeted hers and a slow passionate oral waltz began. With newfound courage, she flipped him on his back and straddled him. Her hair draped to the left side of her body, touching the bed. She smiled and asked him if he was okay. He smiled and said, "I'm fine."

The two went into the early morning hours kissing, caressing, holding, and loving. Every time he tugged to pull her silk pants downward she grabbed them to keep them up. *Sex was not going to be part of the equation this time,* she promised herself.

He respected her wishes.

Around 4:30am, they ended up both falling asleep with her in his arms.

CHAPTER TWENTY-FOUR

~~~~~~

About one o'clock that afternoon the sunlight danced on Ava's eyelids as she awakened on her back. She looked up to the ceiling for a short moment and sprung up. Oma's voice ripped through Ava's subconscious like a European high-speed train. She berated Ava with no empathy. *How could you?! You are a married woman. You need to get the hell out of here. You are playing a dangerous game, young lady, even if you didn't have sex. Married women don't do this. I know you have your suspicions about Uli and his early mornings coming home. But maybe that's just all it is. He could be doing what he says he's doing and he could be just a workaholic. This is how you repay him? What's wrong with you young people? Things don't go your way and you want out? You get stood up a few times and you are ready to throw away years? He's a working man. So what he doesn't let you order your food. Whatever your Opa ordered for me, I ate it. I didn't always want what he ordered. Your Opa and I loved each other until death do you part. Where is your love for Uli? Have you replaced it, child?* Ava remembered promising Oma on her deathbed that she would stay with Uli until death. Oma loved Uli; she was the only reason Opa put up with him. The only time Oma ever deferred from the "Death Do You Part" commitment was when her brother-in-law left Ava's great-aunt and served her papers. Oma told her, "He left you, and you can't make him love you. So pick yourself up and get back up. When you have papers, you can't make him stay. You did everything you could do. He's gone, so you have to live your life." Ava laid in the bed quietly.

Calvin's voice registered. "Good morning, Beautiful. Or should I say, good afternoon?"

"Good afternoon?" She rushed out the bed and collected her things. *Let me get the hell out of here.* She didn't know if she would have the strength to fight off her urges, and she wasn't taking any chances.

"What's wrong, Baby?" He said with a soft and tender touch.

"It's just late and I have to get home." She grabbed her dress that he had re-ironed and hung in the closet for her earlier that morning.

"I thought you said no one was there and you had plenty of time."

"I have some things I need to do at Schwarz." She peeled of the pajamas he'd given her and for a brief moment he saw her full body, sculpted thighs, etched stomach muscles, and delicate hips covered by orange lace panties that he was sure turned into a thong if he had seen her from behind. His body responded to the quick peek at hers. The dress quickly dropped over her shoulders to cover her beauty.

"Don't you want to shower first?"

"No. I'll do that at the gym."

"Okay. Are you mad at me? Did I push too hard?"

"No. Why are you asking me that?"

"You haven't stop once to look me in the eye or slow down one bit. It seems like you have some discomfort."

She stopped and looked him in his hazel brown eyes. Her heart lifted, stopping her breath. She planted the softest peck on his lips she could. She left her lips on his a little longer to savor the moment. In her mind and in her heart, she knew that was the last time she would touch those lips ever again.

"Now, that's more like it. Call me when you get to the gym."

"I will." Man, he's sweet even to the end.

Ava kept her word as soon as she got to the gym. She called while sitting in her car in the parking lot.

The next call was to Uli. Maybe a conversation with him could clear her mind, give her some direction, or even be more powerful than the thoughts she was having about Calvin. She listened to the muffled ringing. Uli often said he didn't call that much because of the poor quality of the phone system where he was located. He claimed the reception was distorted with an awful lot of static. But this time, the call went through. "Mr. Kärcher please, room 271."

Uli finally picked up without letting her say one word.

"Hi, Honey. I'll be there in ten minutes. Don't forget to wear that sexy little black lingerie underneath. You know how I like to see that tight little twenty-two-year-old body of yours. Just think, it's been three years now since I took you into my life."

Ava hung up and burst into angry tears.

"How foolish of me to be worried about the little kissing and touching Calvin and I just did while Uli is making love to a child!" Her voice went from a whimper to yelling. "She's twenty-two! Uli has been cheating with a baby! Well, if this is how you want it, Mr. Kärcher, this is how we are going to do it. There will be divorce papers waiting for you when you get home!"

Ava sped off and went back to the bed and breakfast, but Calvin had already checked out. She walked around the city of St. Augustine until she ended up on Cordova and King streets.

She stumbled upon an enormous castle that had to have been constructed for a king. She decided that this was where she and Calvin would share their first intimate evening.

"Hello, ma'am. Welcome to the Casa Monica. My name is Lauren. May I help you?"

"Yes. I am planning a special weekend for two in two weeks. What would you recommend?"

"I recommend the Anastasia suite. This is our signature suite. It goes for nine hundred and forty dollars a night. As a matter of fact, it's empty right now. Would you like to see it?"

"Yes, I would." Lauren summoned the bellhop over to the desk. "John, would you give the lady a tour of the Anastasia Suite?" He smiled and led her through the five-star hotel's beautiful corridors.

When he opened the double doors into the master room, Ava responded, "I see why this suite is highly recommended. This Spanish decor is magnificently done."

"Ma'am, most people fall in love with this suite at first sight, but it also has a second floor. If you follow me up the spiral staircase to your left, I can show you what I mean," John said gently. When they reached the top of the staircase, there was a beautiful king-sized bed as the centerpoint; the headboard was a large, shiny red oak with deep, intricate carvings. The middle section of the headboard was covered with massive red satin. The bed backed to the wall and faced two ceiling-to-floor widows that gave spectacular views.

"So just think we are looking at these views in the middle of the day. You can imagine how this atmosphere is amplified at night with soft lighting. There is even a turret that you have access to if you walk down that small hall," he said.

"I am truly impressed."

"Well, does that mean you don't want me to show you the bath area? It is simply stunning."

"Oh no! I didn't say that. Please show it to me."

They walked about six feet from the bedroom to another set of Spanish doors that he opened with a boastful, "Wah-lah!"

"Oh my goodness. This is beautiful!"

"Thank you. We are proud of it. It was just renovated last week, so not many people have seen it in this state. The white marble and this eight-foot, porcelain tub with the golden claws are from Italy. This tub was designed with a special outer material that keeps the temperature comfortable for hours. It was made with great care in Milano, Italy. We especially like the fact that the gold faucet is positioned in the middle of the side of the tub. That works perfectly for two people to enjoy a bath together, one person at each end comfortably. We also have a separate rain shower. As you can see, it equally has the high attention to detail for our clients."

"Okay, we can go back to the front desk. I have seen enough." As they walked back to the front desk, Ava felt the beauty of the hotel and became excited about the plans she would soon make.

"Ma'am, did you like the suite?" Lauren asked.

"Yes. It will do just fine. I would like to pay for it now. Is it available Friday in two weeks for the entire weekend?" This would be when Opa and Roger would visit Oma's gravesite in New York. So the timing couldn't be any better.

"That's strange. We just had a cancellation, and it is. This must be your lucky day because normally this time of year there is a long waiting list."

"I would like to just say it's destiny."

~~~~~~

Ava called Calvin after her second surgery of the day. She had to push herself to not think about him during both. Her entire body and soul sung when he answered his cell phone. "Hi, Calvin."

"I'm a little surprised to see your name pop up in my phone."

"Oh, yeah. Why?"

"I thought I saw something in your eyes before you left. And it felt like you were saying goodbye with that kiss. I left the bed and breakfast right after you. I was sick to my stomach. I thought I'd pushed you too hard and I took you too far, too fast to a place you didn't feel comfortable."

"No. I was trying to make it to surgery. Do you have time tonight for dinner?"

"I always have time for you."

"I do have a quick question."

"Please, Ava, ask."

"Did I understand you correctly when you said you have the ability to determine your own schedule at work? And if you want to take a couple of days off, you can without any repercussions?"

"Yes. You are correct. I work because I want to not because I have to. Why do you ask?"

"Some things a girl likes to keep to herself. I'll see you tonight."

~~~~~~

As usual, Calvin was already at the restaurant when she arrived. She walked over to him, placed her hand on his shoulder, and kissed his cheek before he could stand. "That's a welcomed surprise," he said. Once she sat down, he reached in his suit's breast pocket, pulled out a white envelope and gave it to her.

"What's this?"

"Open it."

With a puzzled look, she opened the envelope. "S-T-D and AIDS results?"

"Yes."

"Yes. But I don't understand."

"Last time we were together ,it was intense. We came pretty close to making love. I hope you can tell that I am developing strong feelings for you. Each time I see you, they become stronger and stronger. What is important for me is that you understand that this isn't purely a sexual thing for me."

Calvin wanted it to be clear: she wasn't going to be some woman on his wall of fame. He was serious and hoped she was, too. "I want to share everything I have with you, Ava. There are a lot of things a woman can share with a man. I am thankful for the time that you have given me and for the parts of your life you have openly shared. Although I desire more, I am grateful for that."

"At the risk of being too forward, Ava," he continued while reaching to hold her hand. He took one deep breath and continued, "if you are considering sharing your most prize possession with me, your temple, I would be totally honored to even be considered."

"If that is the case," he pointed to the papers for Ava to look at them again. "I feel you deserve to know that with me you are not risking anything that would harm you."

When Calvin found out her issues with latex. He took it upon himself to get tested by his physician and provide her with the results.

"I guess I just want you to know that I am clear of any S-T-Ds. And I want you to know I am H-I-V negative and I do not have AIDS. I need you to know what you are getting with me if we decide to share something as precious as love making together. Sorry if I am being too forward. I just want your mind to be at ease."

Ava looked him in his eyes and smiled. She placed her hand gently on top of his. And with the softest voice she possessed she said,

"No harm taken. We are both adults, and there is never anything wrong when people act as responsible adults. I really think that it is such a sweet and thoughtful gesture from you. For you to open up to me and to take the initiative and provide me with this personal information, that's a big move on your part. We've known each other for a while now. We've shared a lot."

She folded the papers, placed them back in the envelope, and handed it to him. She leaned over close to his face and whispered, "Well, to answer your question about when and if love making is on our horizon," she looked at his lips then back to his eyes. "Like I said before, there are some things a lady keeps to herself until the time is right." She smiled and closed her eyes.

Their lips met.

CHAPTER TWENTY-FIVE

~~~~~~

D r. Kärcher? Attorney Brown will see you now."

Brown, Brown, and Crane handled all of Opa's and Star Real Estate's legal affairs throughout the world, but the firm was headquartered in Jacksonville.

Melissa Brown, the second partner in the firm, was an ex-swim teammate of Ava. They'd known each other since high school. The fact that Melissa was a woman also played a small role in Ava's decision to use her for the divorce procedures. Ava wanted to keep every aspect of the divorce as discreet and confidential as possible—especially since Opa dealt with William Brown exclusively.

Uli and the firm's third partner, Chip Crane, worked well together. Both shared a take-over-the-world mentality that many people called a Napoleon Complex behind their backs.

"Hello, Ava. What brings you in to the office today?" Melissa said greeting her friend with a hug.

"Hi, Melissa," she said with mixed emotions. "I would like to file for divorce."

Caught off guard, Melissa stood quietly for a moment. She shook her head as if she was waking herself up, "I am sorry to hear that. Can the marriage be reconciled?"

"No. He's been in a relationship with this twenty-two-year-old child for three years and I just found out."

Melissa gestured for Ava to sit in the chair in front of the desk. "Middle-aged men go through this quite often. I must advise you that since you are the wealthier party in the marriage and you're filing, you will be ordered to pay some type of alimony. You must take everything under consideration, such as your position in the firm. You are the only heir to this fortune. Aside from your stock in the company, his attorney would even bring up your income as a surgeon. Uli would more than likely do everything possible to make it seem as if he is the one in destitute and that he will suffer because of all the years he lost. He'll demand to have some type of major compensation."

Melissa sat in the chair next to Ava and continued, "You are a wealthy woman and you can be sure he and his attorney, especially if it's Crane, are going to make it worth their while for a very long time." Ava listened closely and nodded as Melissa advised her. They both knew Uli wasn't short on wealth but without Ava and Opa, his well would quickly dry.

"Given the fact that you two have been married for some time, the court may even demand for you to insure that his lifestyle not be compromised away from what he is accustomed to living. I am pretty certain that the court will rule in his favor for the alimony. To be honest, Ava, my job will be to reduce that dollar amount to a minimum. But it will be hefty."

Ava pounded her fist on the arm of her chair, "I don't care! This guy has made my life hell for some time and now I know why. It all makes sense, all of it!"

"Okay, Ava." Melissa said, giving her friend a moment to settle her emotions, which didn't take long. Ava was stern.

"I will get things started. I will draw up everything and let you take a look at it, and when everything is in order we will then file."

"Melissa, this must stay confidential and between us only."

"Yes, Ava. Not even William will know. You do have attorney-client privilege. That counts even against my husband."

They both smiled. Melissa embraced her and whispered, "It's going to be okay."

That night, before drifting to sleep, Ava determined that she was doing the right thing.

~~~~~~

"Guten Morgen," Opa said as Ava entered the kitchen. She gave him a broad smile and hugged Gertrude who handed her a glass of pineapple juice.

"You know you look like my old granddaughter!" He practically yelled. "You sure have been beaming the past several months. That Uli should stay away on business more often."

"Guten Morgen, Opa. I have been pretty happy lately."

"Are you coming with us to New York? You haven't been to the gravesite for a while now."

"I promise, Opa, next month for sure. I have a previous engagement that I must fulfill."

"Okay. I'll tell her you'll be there next month." Opa said, committing Ava to the visit.

"Thanks, Opa. Have a safe trip." She sealed their agreement with a kiss on his cheek.

Her day in the hospital was filled with meetings, audits, and patient reports which made the hours speed by and helped her temper her the excitement shooting through her body.

As usual, Calvin was at A1A when she arrived, waiting patiently.
"Ready?" He asked.

"Yes."

Calvin opened the door for her to walk in, and she stopped him.

"We aren't eating here tonight."

"Then where are we going, Gorgeous?" His smile made her heart quiver and she made a point to remember that feeling.

"Follow me."

The two walked down King Street until they reached the intersection at Cordova Street and stopped. She looked to the left and right and said, "We're dining here."

"Here? At the Casa Monica."

"Yes, here, the Casa Monica."

Calvin opened the glass door and she walked in to the dinning area.

"Calvin Hollaway party of two," Ava said proudly.

"Right this way." The maître d' directed them to a secluded room. He pulled back the curtains to a private dinning area that could seat twenty people for an intimate meal. The dimly lit space was decorated with tasteful Spanish artwork covering all walls.

On the wall hung a twenty-foot oil painting of a Spanish woman wearing a black sleeveless dress. A red flower adorned her hair and she held an open, red fan behind her head.

To Calvin's surprise, only one table and two chairs sat in the middle of the entire area. When the curtains closed, the soft sounds of a strumming guitar came from the young teenager playing Flamenco music.

"Here are your menus. What would you like to drink?"

"Water for me," Calvin said.

"I'll have your sweetest house wine, please."

"Very well. I'll be back with your drinks and to take your orders."

As soon as he walked away, Calvin leaned in and whispered, "This is amazing, Beautiful."

"Sit back and relax, the entire night is for you to enjoy."

The waiter returned and they ordered their meals. After the meal the waiter came back to check on them.

"Did you two enjoy your meals?"

"Yes. It was simply fabulous," Ava replied.

"Will there be any dessert?"

"No thank you. But I would like a little more wine."

"I'll have another glass of water, please."

"Very well."

"Are you okay, Ava?"

"I am fine. Just have a little jitters."

"Jitters for what? You don't need to have jitters with me."

She reached in her purse and pulled out and envelope and handed it to Calvin. He smiled as he took the envelope. "I feel you deserve to know everything I know about you. I, too, have a clean bill of health. You won't be the only one cumming with a clear conscience."

They both gave each other a knowing smirk.

Calvin pushed his chair back and crossed his arms. "You know, lady, I feel a little violated. First you feed me and then you want to, ummm, well, no, I guess I can't say that. We've really never made love."

No we haven't. But we will tonight. Ava thought. Ava reached in her purse again and pulled out two key cards. Calvin sat, frozen with a partially opened mouth.

"This is your key, when you get to the elevators just tell the bellhop you're going to the Anastasia Suite. I hope you opened your weekend like we discussed." She stood from the table and gave him a wink. "Give me a few minutes to freshen up." She gave him a quick peck on the lips. "See you in a few."

"Okay," Calvin said taking in a deep breath. "I'll just take care of the bill first."

"No need. Everything has been covered," she said as she walked out the room. Calvin finished his water and calmed himself by listening to a final song by the talented guitarist. Then, he headed to the Anastasia Suite.

He slowly unlocked the door and walked into the palatial suite, a setting fit for a king. Ava stood in the center of the room, wearing a sheer, white-laced bustier with matching panties. He allowed the doors to close behind him.

Two white garter belts were snapped from the bottom of the bustier to the top of her thigh-high nylon spandex. She wore a two-inch pearl choker. Standing boldly in four-inch heels, she gestured with her right index finger for him to come in.

He walked over to her and took his time to embrace her. He kissed her ear and whispered, "You are simply stunning. I love what you're wearing and the way you smell. Creed's Love in White smells so good on an amazing woman."

"Thank you. I'm so glad you love my fragrance."

Calvin smiled as he nodded. He knew the fragrance intimately. He remembered Déjà explaining to him that royalty wore it, so she would wear it for her king.

For the first time the thought of her in Ava's presence didn't bring guilt or shame. He felt her approval.

Ava took his hands from around her, "Let me give you a personal tour of the place. It's simply fabulous!"

"You might want to be careful."

"Huh?"

"The moment you grabbed my hand I felt my friend I call Trouble damn near double in size."

"Why do you call him that?"

"Because when he's around he's all about finding trouble."

She smiled and looked down towards Trouble, licking her lips. He had never seen her do that but the suggestion was enough to build up his confidence.

The two toured the suite hand-in-hand. He lagged behind her just to reach his left hand into his pants and do some much needed adjusting.

Ava smiled. "Is everything okay with Mr. Trouble?"

"Oh yeah, he's fine."

"This artwork you see here was designed solely for this room. Let me show you the upstairs," she said as she led him up the spiral staircase.

"Man! Now that's a king's bed! What does the bathroom look like? Tell me there's a large tub." She pointed in the direction of the bathroom. Calvin headed straight for the shower.

He came out of the shower dripping wet with a towel wrapped around his waist. "I couldn't get out that shower fast enough," he admitted. "All I could think about was how sexy you look on the other side of the door." He explained, holding his clothes neatly folded in front of Trouble. She looked quizzically at the clothes.

"I guess my O-C-D is getting the best of me." He shrugged his shoulders and looked for a place to sit them. "I can't stand wrinkles in my clothes. I've been that way for as long as I can remember. My family has always kidded me about that."

When he placed them on the floor, she finally saw Trouble for the first time. "Oh...My...Gosh," she whispered loudly. She expected him to be in good shape but when he came out, his physique was simply remarkable.

All nine and a half inches pointed directly at her with a slight hook. Calvin pulled her close to him. He placed a soft kiss on her lips that she intentionally stopped time to savor. The next thing Ava knew she was in the air. He lifted her effortlessly. Instinctively, she wrapped her legs around his waist and became very nervous. His power surprised her. She whispered in his ear. "I need to be honest with you. By no means of the imagination am I a virgin, but it's been awhile, Calvin. My body is closely built."

Calvin stared deep into her sapphire eyes until she felt him reach her soul and tickle it. "I'm not going to hurt you, that I can promise you." Barely able to breathe she listened and inhaled every word from his fresh breath. *He must keep Scope in his pocket.* She thought. Her mind was racing in all directions. She was more nervous than she thought she would be. But she loved the way her olive skin looked against his deep brown.

"We're going to be fine. We can lay here together and you can fall asleep in my arms if you want, there's no pressure."

"Are you saying you don't want to make love to me?"

"Sweetie. That is exactly what I am saying. I've never wanted to make love to you. I have dreamed of making love with you."

"I want to make love with you, too."

"Listen. We have this place for the entire weekend, right? Then there's no rush. If not this weekend then whenever you're really ready."

He gently stood her at the edge of the bed.

He walked across the room to a cabinet hidden within the wall and connected his phone to the suite's sound system. He selected Teddy Pendergrass from his playlist. It started playing one of his favorites: "Come On Over to My Place."

"May I have this dance?"

"Yes, you may."

Slowly and erotically they danced, her face rested on his chest as the two moved their lower extremities from side to side. He then turned her around with her back to him. He moved her hair to the side and kissed her softly on the back of her neck. Her eyes closed whe[n] she felt the softness of his lips and the warmth of his breath.

He whispered in her ear, "This is my favorite part of the night. You are not under any kind of pressure. If I do anything that doesn't please you, I'll understand if you say no."

She turned to face him. "There's no way in hell I'm saying no. Being with you makes me feel like I'm making love for the very first time. I feel like a little girl inside. Here I am wearing this for you but I don't want you to see me completely naked and in all my glory, this is crazy. I can't explain it but it's a little embarrassing."

"I am a man of my word and we don't have to do anything that makes you uncomfortable. You can keep what you have on and we can just lay in this beautiful bed with this amazing view and talk until we fall asleep."

She gave him a long kiss and said, "I want to try."

"Okay. But if you feel any discomfort, say the word and I'll stop."

He kneeled at her feet and took his time helping her out of her pumps. He took his time to massage her feet. Slowly he worked his way up her legs. He noticed her muscles tensing. He looked up at her, "Let me know, Baby." Her eyes were closed and she nodded her head slowly.

Piece by piece, her trust grew more and more. The shyness and her nervousness slowly eased. She watched his back muscles clinch and relax as his hands massaged her legs and thighs. She really couldn't remember the last time she saw a man completely naked other than Uli. And this was definitely not Uli.

He undressed her as he slowly massaged every inch of her body. He took his time, focusing on the feel of her skin and the heat lifting from her.

Everything about Calvin made her feel giddy, from his strength to his physique, even the size of his male anatomy. He kissed her again and her butterflies disappeared. He placed his next kiss on her neck, then he traveled slowly southward. With his tongue stopping to suck between her breast, then down to suck her right rib, and back across her body to suck just above her navel, he made her feel special and desired. Completely lost in the moment, she closed her eyes and just let him explore her with his hands, lips, breath, and tongue.

He made his way to the crown of Ava's left hip. His breath floated across her little lady she named Missy. His lips soon followed. Slowly kissing and sucking, he drove her close to the brink of insanity. With the slight push of his hand, he gently placed her clitoris in his mouth and rested his hands under her behind. Slowly he lifted Ava's erection with his tongue and rocked it from side to side, in and out of his mouth, and gently tugging it with his lips. He masterfully sped and slowed his rhythm, forcing Ava to arch her back as high as she could. Her moans were steady. Her eyes closed. Unexpectedly, her stream flowed as she reached her first peak.

With newfound bravery, she rolled him on his back. He felt so safe, so familiar, so right. She straddled him, locked in on his hazel brown eyes and stared, looking deeply into his soul. There, she saw love. She kissed his forehead, between his eyes.

She grabbed her hair and pulled it to the side. She gently kissed his collarbone and slowly started her journey southward. She took a short stop at his right nipple, kissing and licking it. She gently caught it between her teeth and bit down quick and stopped. She did the same to the left nipple causing Calvin to groan. Trouble was to the point of being unbendable. He had not felt an erection that intense since his last night in Kuwait.

Kissing and making her way down his abdomen, Ava slowly wrapped her small, soft, warm hands around Trouble. She pulled back her flowing blonde hair once again before putting her lips slowly and gently around his shaft. As it slowly disappeared in her mouth, Calvi closed his eyes and moaned. For a moment, time stopped within him as he laid in a well of pleasure. He took in Ava's touch, her kissing, the sounds of her pleasing him. His heart was full and Trouble was ready to explode. Calvin pulled Ava up and they switched positions.

Passionately kissing and touching each other, Ava's body spread as Calvin entered her.

She let out a gasp and a breathy, "Oh, Yes!"

After thirteen minutes of Calvin's deep stroking, she released a river flow. With each thrust harder and faster, their bodies climbed and adjusted to the love making until they both climaxed.

Calvin brushed her hair away from her face then looked in her eyes as she said, "I think I'm falling in love."

He stopped and kissed her with all the passion that welled in his body. "I know I am, Ava."

CHAPTER TWENTY-SIX

~~~~~~

Calvin submerged most of his body into the porcelain tub of bubbles and warm water. He gazed up at the ceiling with his head resting just over the edge. Both arms relaxed on the side as he replayed the last eighteen hours with Ava.

Déjà's voice broke his trance. *Yeah. It feels good doesn't it, Calvin? To love, to touch, to feel again? I'm so happy for you, Baby.*

"I must admit it does, Déjà. It's been so long."

You deserve it, Calvin. You are doing what is normal.

"So how much did you see?" He wondered.

I saw enough to know that German sister brought it! She chuckled. *And in the Anastasia suite, too? If you are going to be with a king, then you treat him like a king. I am not mad at her, and I am proud of you for releasing me.*

Calvin smiled. "She reminds me so much of you. We danced under the stars to our song."

"Don't. Don't do that, Calvin. I know we have a lot in common. Even down to wearing the same perfume but she must have her own journey with you. Your relationship is with her now and she deserves to have

you with her at a hundred percent—not with the me you see in her. My energy will always be present for you, but it's you and her now, Calvin."

For the first time, Déjà looked above her left shoulder and gave a smile as a yellow and white light opened from the ceiling. She looked at Calvin. *I love you with all of me. Thank you.* She said before vanishing. This time he felt it was final.

And he knew he would be alright.

CHAPTER TWENTY-SEVEN

~~~~~~

It's Monday morning and Calvin had just finished his normal routine when the phone rang.

"Hello."

"Tell me about your father. Was he a farmer?" Calvin broke into a loud laughter. He and Cheryl loved that passage from "The Silence of the Lambs."

"What's up, Sis?"

"I just found funding for you."

"What?"

"Yep. I wrote a grant for you!" Cheryl screamed through the phone. "It's to house all your veterans. It's called No More Homeless Vets, and you got it!"

"Man, that's great!" Calvin pumped his fist in celebration.

"I didn't want to tell you until it was approved."

"Dad is going to be so happy. He always said he wanted to find a way to help the ones who gave so much. And you know Mom is going to be all in, too. They've sat on the board all this time without the organization doing anything, they will be glad to finally have a real project for the J.W.T. Hollaway Foundation."

Calvin's brain jumped into action. "Well, Sis, I am not going in today after that news. I'm headed to Mom and Pop. I want to see their faces when I tell them."

"Okay. Don't forget to video it with your phone. I want to see, too."

~~~~~~

Calvin walked into his parent's home and his mom noticed something different about him. This is the third time in at least six months that he looked like the man she had raised.

"Mom. Pop. I have great news! We have been awarded a grant to help homeless vets."

His father smiled as he walked up to him and shook his hand. "Son, this is great! We get to help people who answered the call. This has been the family legacy; it's been our calling. We've long since been helping and involved. We are doing this!"

"Calvin," his mom's tone was serious. "I know my baby and there is something going on with you. What is it?"

His mother looked into his eyes as Calvin tried to look away. "Oh my! You are seeing someone."

Calvin let go of a small grin.

"Is it the doctor who saved that passenger? Have you spent some real time together? Does she like you? When's the next date?" If he didn't stop her, his mom would question him all day.

"Mom. Yes, we have been out and we see each other regularly, but I would never kiss and tell."

Mrs. Hollaway looked at her husband and they both chuckled. "Okay, Calvin," she said, "but do tell us when you're ready."

"Mom, I promise, you will be one of the first to know if this goes anywhere." Calvin stood up to leave. "I have a lot to do before tonight."

"What's going on tonight? Another date?" She quipped.

Calvin placed his index finger on his lips. "What did we just agree on, Mrs. Hollaway?"

She smiled and said, "Okay. Have fun."

"Oh, mom, I've been seeing your Bird of Paradise bouquets all over the Mayo Clinic, at the entrance of a few restaurants, and over at the pet crematory. I even saw the van delivering a bouquet to the principal at the Carter G. Woodson Academy. I love what you and Kenicia are doing to expand and market. Ya'll make a great team." He kissed his mom and left.

~~~~~~

Ava came into the waiting area as Calvin sat patiently. "Mr. Hollaway?"

"Yes."

"You can come with me."

Calvin got up and followed her as everyone in the waiting area watch them leave. They disappeared down the hall and into Ava's office. Once the door closed, he pulled her close and kissed her as if he hadn't seen her in years. After gathering herself from the kiss, she asked, "Is everything okay?"

Calvin nodded.

"You really look great in scrubs, Doc."

Ava smiled. "Thanks, Calvin. I bet you say that to all the female physicians." He smiled and shook his head.

Her office had a shower and dressing room. "I'm going to get out of these scrubs and jump in the shower and I'll be right out." He resisted the urge to invite himself to join her, but he wasn't totally sure of what liberties he could take. Jacksonville had come a long way but race relations were still tenser than they should've been. A White woman loving a Black man still brought stares and insolent treatment. He in no way wanted his behavior to harm her or her career. Instead, he stood by the window looking at a photo of Silva and Opa framed in a heave emerald green and silver case.

Ava emerged more stunning with the sweet smell of Love in White. She wore a spaghetti-strap, flower sundress with yellow sandals. Calvin looked at her manicured and freshly painted small toes. "You look great," he said quickly.

"What do you have planned for us tonight, Calvin?"

He opened the door and whispered in her ear as she walked by, "I have just the place."

The two walked through the winding corridors of the hospital and into the parking garage to Calvin's Tesla. He opened the passenger door then walked over to the driver's side and got in. He turned the key to the two position.

"So where are we going?" Ava asked again.

Calvin turned the radio on to the Delilah Radio Show and reached across her lap to catch her hand. He lifted her left hand and kissed it. "I am so blessed to be here with you. This feels so right." He stared into her eyes. "Do you know what I am looking at?"

"Yes. Me."

"I am looking into your beautiful, piercing sapphire eyes, and I see my cure. I know this may seem as if I am moving too fast. But I have had a long head start. I've been alone and sick every since the day I lost Déjà. I never thought I would ever find anyone else. I stopped looking, but you stole my heart when you came into my life. I know we've made love only once but that is just the point. We made love. Every stroke, every kiss, every lick, and every touch came from my heart. We did things I never thought about doing."

Ava squeezed his hand and smiled in agreement.

"I haven't been with another woman, and it's not because the opportunity didn't present itself. It was my choice. I guess I was waiting for the right one. I was waiting for you.

"At the risk of sounding selfish, if our Heavenly Father was here right now and said one of us had to come home, I would beg him to take me. I would tell him, 'As Your child, Lord, please take me!' Ava, I don't ever want to know what it feels like to walk the earth without a heart ever again."

He closed his eyes and kissed her softly on the lips.

"I know what love smells like. I know what love looks like. I know how love tastes. I know what I hear coming from my heart. I know what I feel."

Ava took the opening to share her feelings. "I know exactly what you are saying, Calvin. If I can be a hundred percent honest with you and tell you, I have always wanted a man like you. I have dreamed and prayed to have a man who would love me and be beside me. That man is definitely you. I, too, feel you with all five senses. We are not moving too fast because this has been my prayer even as a little girl."

Ava slowly kissed him and touched him. Her hand felt like hot coal against his body.

"Young lady, you are going to find yourself eye-to-eye with Trouble if you keep that up."

"I certainly hope so."

Before they realized it, Delilah's show was going off the air, and Calvin knew that meant it was midnight.

"Can you believe it's this late?" Ava said with a big smile. "No I can't, Hun. I told you before what really good company you are, Sweet Lady." Calvin drove Ava to her car a few lanes over. She got into the car and rolled down the window.

"Calvin. What do you say we go by The St. John's Town Center and do a little window-shopping. I need to walk off some of this energy? Besides, I'm not ready for tonight to end, I'm having such a great time."

"That's cool. I'll follow you."

~~~~~~

They pulled up in front of the Apple Store. Calvin got out of his car and opened her door. "Calvin, there's no one out here."

"It's a little after midnight, Hun."

"I want you to know I feel so good with you I feel completely safe with you. You're like my superman."

A shy boyish smile took over his face. The two stopped in front of the Victoria Secret store and looked through the window. "I would love to see you in that white outfit over there in the corner." Ava looked and nodded.

"Look at the pink one up front, over there to the right. I wouldn't mind you taking that one off of me. You've seen me in white already."

Calvin smiled.

"Look over there. Do you see that black little number? What do you think about that? Would you ever wear something like it?"

"Yes. With four-inch heels walking straight to you. What if I brought some handcuffs with me? How would that make you feel?" She waited for him to answer.

"Ava, Black guys don't do handcuffs that well," he said, half jokingly. "But if that adds flavor to your soup, I am down with it. I'll try anything with you at least once. If we like it, we can do it again."

The two walked holding hands and came to the center of an intimate courtyard framed by small trees and bushes that created an ambiance of a little green oasis. He noticed his mom's Bird of Para-

154

dise arranged in two pots across the courtyard. *Mom is everywhere.* He thought and considered it a confirmation that her shop belonged in this complex.

"Did you really mean what you said about the cuffs, Calvin?"

They stood near the couryard's wicker chairs and broad love seats with bright yellow pillows. "Yes, Hun. Why do you ask?"

"This evening we have bared our souls. I feel comfortable enough tonight to share two fantasies I have. I never thought I would share this let alone ask someone to help me with it. I feel I can trust you but on one hand, I don't want you to think badly about me. May I?"

Calvin softly placed his hands on each side of her face and he kissed her forehead. "You can ask me anything. I mean anything. You don't ever have to think I would have bad thoughts about you or look down on you. It's me and you, Hun, from here on out."

Ava took a big gulp and went for it. "Here it goes. I have this fantasy about you raping me. I thought about this but never found anyone I would trust to ask. The first time we talked and I found out you were raised by so many women who you love greatly, I considered asking you then."

"I. I don't know about that." With eyes bucked and an uncertain half-smile, Calvin said, "I wouldn't know how to do that."

"You see it's not really rape, it's me giving you permission to completely take me. Your sensitivity and gentleness make me feel so safe and trusting of you that I want you to be the guy I experience this with."

She rubbed the muscles on his arm, hoping her touch would make him relax. Calvin slowly shook his head, a grimacing look rose across his face. "Back in the day, I would be killed for even thinking this."

"Not in Germany," she replied. "Calvin, the more time we spent together allowed me to see how much of a gentleman you are, so the fantasy crossed my mind again. At the bed and breakfast when you said we could just lay there and not do anything. And the moment I felt your strength, I was all in on trusting you."

"Wait," Calvin said, obviously collecting his thoughts. "First of all, I want to tell you how honored I am that you chose me. Some guys have it all wrong and think we make the selection but you decide whom you will offer your sacred space to," he said, watching her eyes. "Making love with you is the sweetest thing I know, Ava. You can trust me and I am in. I don't think badly about anything that will make you happy."

They stood there quietly for a moment before sitting down. She sat in the chair directly in front of him and tucked her foot under her dress.

Calvin tilted his head then said, "But you said two fantasies. I want to fulfill them both."

"Calvin, I am glad you feel that way. I was really nervous about what your answer would be," she said with a prodigious smile.

She got out of the chair that was directly in front of him and pulled her dress up high enough not to rip it but low enough to hide her bare behind. Calvin could smell the coconut oil Ava massaged into Missy. Climbing on top of his lap, she straddled him then placed her knees on the yellow cushion right at each of his sides. Instinctively, he caught her waist, and she went straight for his zipper.

By the time she freed Trouble from his navy slacks and blue OKON briefs, Missy was already drooling.

"The first time we tangled you got the best of me, Mr. Hollaway. But this time, I'm ready." She couldn't wait to fully mount him.

"Damn. Hun, there's someone watching us," he whispered in her ear. "Hun. There's someone watching us."

"Fuck Me," she whispered through forced teeth.

Did she just say what I think she said?

"There is someone over there watching us."

"Does it bother you that they're watching? Trouble don't care and neither do I."

"If you are okay with it, I am, too."

She kissed his ear, grabbing the lobe with her front teeth. "Fuck me hard!" She said in his ear. She leaned back to sit up straight and bared her hips down to pull Calvin deeper into her. She looked him in the eye and saw satisfaction on his face, "Let's give them something to look at! Fuck me harder. Let them see how hard you can fuck me!"

Her voice served as a jockey's whip with each request. He thrust her harder and deeper, tightening the grip on her hips with each stroke and at each request.

"That's right, fuck me like that! The harder you thrust me in the air the faster I'm going to pound back down!"

Through gritted teeth he said, "I love this mouth of yours, it's giving me such a rush."

Calvin held on to her hips as she rode him like a broncobuster. After she reached her climax she had just enough energy to lay her head on his shoulder and feel the light from his orgasm flood through her body. They held each other until their hearts stopped racing and the sweat dried on her back. "Are they still watching?"

"No. They left."

She slowly peeled off of him giving him space to close up his pants. As they stood together, she said, "That was the other fantasy: to make love in public. To have someone watch, well, that was a bonus."

They walked back to their cars, and she left like nothing happened. Calvin lingered around to see the vacant storefronts and to select the perfect one for his mother.

CHAPTER TWENTY-EIGHT

~~~~~~

At 2 a.m., right outside the city of Prague in the Czech Republic, Uli sat behind his desk full of himself, as he spoke. "First of all, I would like to start by congratulating you both on this crop you've selected. I couldn't have found two better business partners if I tried."

Uli pulled out the corporate checkbook and paid a handsome finder's fee to both his associates. He meticulously signed each check *H. Lang.*

"My policy is when you find great employees, you hold on to them by paying them their value. You two are worth every cent you see on your checks."

After reading the check, the partner with the scar could not hide his enthusiasm. "Man! Mr. Uli, thanks so much!" The other goon chimed in after reviewing his check.

"You two were right, and where I come from when a man is right, you pay him for it."

The guy with the long scar couldn't wait to toot his own horn. "Uli, we knew you would be happy with this pick of young ones. There isn't a one over the age twenty-one, each one more beautiful than the next. They will all fetch a nice sum."

Uli replied. "Yes. This is going to put our company on the map. As a matter of fact, we are going to be at the top after our showing. I even found two for myself."

"Two?" The strong, silent partner asked.

"Yes, two. There are two words that peek my interest every time. When I hear 'new' and 'young,' I am all in. Let me tell you something, if you see a girl over thirty with me, it can only be one of three reasons: I am married to her, we are fighting, or I am holding her for the police." Uli arrogantly replied.

Their loud laughter was interrupted by a knock on the door. The silent man went to check it out. "Uli, it's your girl." Uli placed his checkbook in the desk's middle drawer and said, "Let her in."

She walked in quickly, smiling at Uli. She was happy to see him.

"Guys, we need to be alone," Uli said, and the men left.

"Darling, have a seat." She sat in the chair in front of his desk. "We will be leaving soon." Uli informed her.

"I need to say goodbye to my family," she stood up quickly.

Uli stopped her. "There has been a change in plans. You aren't going back with us."

Rage swept across her face. "I can't do this anymore, U.K! You were supposed to leave your wife! We were to be married already!"

Uli tried to reason. "Sometimes things take a little longer than normal."

"Maybe things would speed up if Městské policie knew where all those young girls disappeared to and who was taking them." She had him cornered. It was time he learned that love and loyalty cost, and he can't promise a girl one thing and snatch it away.

"Now, we don't need to invite anyone into something you know so little about," he said, walking across the room. She knew Uli loved his classical music, so when he walked over to turn up the volume, she waited and let him listen to "The Flying Dutchman-Overture," by Richard Wagner. She had learned to enjoy the sounds and the expressions on Uli's face as he indulged. But this time, instead of watching him, she turned her head to look away and to temper her anger.

In an instant, she felt his tie wrap around her neck and noticed the music was louder than ever. She tried to grab the tie. Her feet swung, kicking the desk for freedom but Uli's grip was fierce and unlike that of the small man she thought loved her. In less than two minutes, he had strangled the life out of her.

He walked over to the music and hummed the final cords before turning the volume down. He knocked twice on the wall and the goons returned.

"Get rid of her, but do it tastefully. After that is done, meet me at the airport. We are getting the hell out of this country, back to the U.S.A."

"Yes, sir."

After some tense negotiating and paying a few penalties, Uli was able to adjust their return flight for a Friday return.

~~~~~~

"Hallo, Opa. Ich bins."

"Hallo, Ava."

"How are things going at Oma's gravesite?"

"It looks great. That Roger is so much help. He oversaw all of the floral changes and cleaned up the headstone. You would be proud."

"I can't wait to see it for myself, Opa. Roger is so good to us.," she smiled and took in a deep breath. "When are you returning home?"

"We won't get back until the beginning of the next week. We're going to go to the beach house when we arrive. I want to dedicate time to review beach branches." Opa asked her to hold on as he coughed to clear his throat. "Have you spoken with Uli lately? He sure is spending a considerable amount of time in Europe. He isn't committed to the firm or his new project. He's not loyal. He's lazy; he lacks focus." At any other time, Ava would have found the perfect words to mollify Opa's frustrations. But with the divorce filings in motion and her heart full of Calvin, she really had no rebuttal.

"Look at Roger's loyalty. It has been evident since we met him as a young boy, Ava. As an American, Roger has shown the heart of a German more than Uli whose blood and bones are native," he said.

Ava listened intently and Opa's sudden tirade against Uli refueled her anger over the affair and the neglect.

"I am going to make a point to address this when I get back." Opa stopped and suddenly softened his voice. "Have I told you how proud I am of you? And you should be, too. Becoming a surgeon was no small feat. Your business acumen is not to be overlooked either. The purchase and renaming of Schwarz and rebuilding your team showed you are a brilliant, natural leader with keen insight. You should continue to trust that about yourself, my dear." Opa sensed the sorrow in her silence.

"Ava, listen to me and forever remember what I am about to say. If you don't ever remember anything else, remember this: something always has to die in order for something else to live." He stopped and waited for his words to stick with her. "Don't let bad partnerships kill you."

He hung up.

Gertrude walked in the parlor as soon as Ava hung up with Opa. She noticed dried tear tracks on Ava's face.

"What's wrong, Ava?"

"Opa said something has to die for something else to live." Gertrude smiled after she heard those words.

"I told your Opa about the time when I was a little girl and my poodle died. I walked in the backyard and saw vultures eating her. They were almost done. I ran back in the house crying, trying to find something to kill the vultures with. My Papa stopped me and told me those very same words. As a matter of fact that is what made me want to go to college. My family never went passed the fifth grade. I decided to kill that history for my family so that our next generations could live," she said.

Master Lang was actually listening to me. Another smile showed up on her face. Gertrude was about to walk away when Ava called her back.

"Auntie Gert, I don't know how you do it."

"Do what?" Gertrude asked.

"Stay in this big house most of the time alone."

Gertrude sat down. "You all have become my family, my world. I noticed your unhappiness for years. You looked like a caged bird. But now you appear to have found a new, genuine source of life and happiness and peace. I am so glad to see it again. I don't know what it is but I am glad you have it back, child. Soon you will fly." Gertrude kissed Ava on the forehead and said, "I got to go. I don't want the food to burn." Both laughed as Gertrude stood and walked away.

Ava's mind returned to Calvin. She needed to talk to him. She needed to tell him the truth about her and Uli, about his affair, and about the upcoming divorce. She also knew she would need to explain why she hadn't told him a year ago when they had their first dinner. But the truth was, she wasn't ready to lose him. She knew Calvin would see her lying by omission as disrespect, and he would end the relationship immediately.

This was the last weekend Ava would have to enjoy with Calvin before Uli and Opa returned home. It was going to be total chaos when the divorce procedures started. She knew things were going to drastically change and seeing Calvin was not going to be possible for a while. The mere thought of that sent trimmers through her body. She needed Calvin to make a house call—especially since she had buried her battery-operated friend, Roscoe. An emergency housecall was a necessity. After one more weekend of lovemaking and her fantasy fix satisfied, she would come completely clean with everything, she convinced herself. *I'll tell him everything right after he takes care of me—and Missy—one more time. Then I'll pray for the best.*

Ava slowly and passionately wrote down her deep dark fantasy on a perfectly squared, crème-colored stationery with scarlet embroidery along the edges.

> *Calvin, since you are so strong I want to feel more of that. I want you to take me! I don't care how much I scream and say, 'No! Please stop!' The more I beg you to stop, the more I want you to keep going. I am so going to enjoy this! The only way you should stop is if I use the safe words. Those words will be Bird of Paradise. When I say that, you can go back to being a gentleman.*

She called Calvin, hoping it wasn't too late for him to come over for a little role playing and a long overdue confession session. The confession would be the most difficult.

"Hello." Calvin answered the call.

"Hi, Calvin."

"Hello, Ava." His voice was deeper than normal. She could tell she had awakened him.

"I know it's late. I am sorry for waking you."

"No. It's okay. What's wrong?"

"I need to talk. I have something that just can't wait. I need to be face-to-face with you."

Calvin sat up in the bed. "Honey, It's almost 2 a.m."

"I know exactly what time it is." She hesitated, then said, "That's why I need a visit from you and Trouble."

Calvin smiled. "Give me the address; I am on my way."

"Okay. I need one other thing if that's okay."

"I'm having a rush right now. Of course, what is it?"

"When you get here you'll see two mailboxes. One will be on the side of the road and the other one is a homemade mailbox that I want you to go to. There won't be a doubt in your mind when you see it. It's close to the house. You'll know that's the one. It'll be to your left when you're walking up to the house. You'll find a letter I wrote for you. Read this letter carefully and do exactly as it says. I mean, exactly! If you don't want to, just call me from your cell after you read the letter. I will be okay with that, too. But I hope you are okay with my request."

Calvin put the address in his GPS and arrived at the mansion quickly.

~~~~~~

Uli stood in the Jacksonville International Airport completely exhausted from the nineteen-hour flight. Standing at the baggage claim, he watched his luggage come around the conveyor belt for the fourth time. But he did not move.

"Sir. Sir? Is everything okay?"

"Yes. Why do you ask?"

"That's the fourth time that luggage has came around, and there's no one else waiting but you."

"Oh, thanks," he said, "Yes, that's mine. What time is it here?"

"It's two forty five."

"Man. I just want to get home."

"Sir, I can help you with that. I'm the best sky cab around."

"I know it's late but is there any way that I can hire a car?"

"Yes, sir. We'll take you where you need to go. This gentleman needs your services, Donald."

"I'll take those bags for you, sir. Where are you going?"

"Avondale."

"Okay, sir. I'll get you there in a hurry."

~~~~~~

Calvin parked and walked to the homemade mailbox Ava described. He read the request and with each letter of every word a sensation traveled from his brain downward, giving him a pulsating, unbendable erection that extended to his navel.

Oh, hell, yeah! I am so with that!

When he opened the front door, he heard a loud, strange type of cuckoo chime. That startled him at first but it only sounded off once. *Man! That's going to take some getting use to.*

He closed the front door and the chime sounded off once again. The house was dark. Calvin froze in place to allow his eyes to adjust in the darkness. He thought about calling out her name but knew that would ruin the fantasy.

At that moment, Ava switched on a soft light in her walk-in closet that cut through the darkness like a razor. He followed the path of the light that helped him to hurry to the bedroom. He waited outside the door as he pretended a rapist would do, lurking and waiting until she came out of her walk-in closet and turned off the light.

Calvin stood still and forced his eyes to adjust to the darkness once again. He focused on the moonlight shining through the entire back wall that was made of glass, facing the river. It illuminated the room and cast enough shadows for him to follow through on her request.

She took off her robe and draped it across a chair. She wore the sexy black outfit they saw in the Victoria Secret window with lace boy shorts and a matching black-lace, strapless bra. Calvin stood hidden in the darkness.

She turned on a small night light and sat down to brush her hair in front of a gigantic mirror. Her grace and beauty paralyzed him for a few minutes. The small seductive show and anticipation made him feel like a dirty little boy being a peeping Tom.

While taking off his clothes, for some strange reason, he remembered a phrase his grandmother said to him when he was about four years old: "Take off everything you didn't come in the world with." He folded his clothes in a neat pile and sat them on the floor.

After brushing her hair, she turned off the small light and walked over to close the curtains. Her heart raced with anticipation. She felt him near. She could smell the lemongrass lotion he wore and the Scope on his breath. Her breast tinkled and her skin awakened, anxious for his touch.

Calvin ran up behind her and grabbed her, placing one hand over her mouth and with the other arm lifting her off the seat.

She kicked and struggled to get away. He threw her on the bed and pinned her down. He snatched off her panties as she fought to get away. He snapped her bra which hung on one latch. Looking deeply into her eyes, he stopped. Ava locked into his eyes and shook her head slowly, as one tear raced down the side of her head. He continued as she slowly gave him an encouraging nod. A smile took over her face as she let out a scream at the top of her lungs, "No! Please stop! Please!"

He pried open her legs and forced himself inside her.

She closed her eyes and made a loud, deep gasping sound, but to Calvin it was, oh, so feminine. It was as if she had been emerged in water for a long time and came up in a nick of time for breath.

Calvin was completely caught up in the moment. His erection never felt this hard in his life. Her screams to stop were muffled by his racing heart that latched on to her moans of pleasure that told him she wanted more. For Calvin, nothing else mattered.

~~~~~~

"Thanks so much, Donald. Let me get your card. The next time I fly in, I want to use your service. I also have some upscale clients who I need to provide transportation for from time to time. Would you be interested in marrying up with me in a business venture?"

"Yes, sir. I have six cars and can get more if need be." Donald got out of the car and went around to open Uli's door.

"That's great to know. I will be in touch." Uli gave Donald a generous tip and walked to the front door. Fumbling to use his key, he leaned on the door and it opened.

Hmm, that's strange; it's not locked. He turned the knob and pushed the door. He heard Ava screaming and begging for her life.

He grabbed his cell phone to call the police and backed outside the house.

"I just arrived home and someone broke in our house and is inside! He's attacking my wife! Please hurry! We live in Avondale on the river!"

He shouted the address and demanded that they hurry. He turned on the phone's voice recorder. *I don't know what is going to happen but if something does happens to me, whoever plays this will be able to hear.*

Uli walked quietly back inside to the terrifying and gut-wrenching pleas from his wife. He heard an object banging against the wall. *I am not going to let him kill her!* He grabbed his Louisville Slugger that sat in the corner of his home office and headed towards the bedroom. He saw the bruit silhouette mounted on top of his wife and heard her constant screams and the bed banging against the wall. It was too much to take in. Uli took a quick, careful aim and swung for Calvin's head.

Through clenched teeth, Ava murmured, "I love the way you're raping me!"

A loud crack ripped through the room, vibrating through Ava's ears and body when all two hundred and five pounds of Calvin's muscular body collapsed on top of her. Uli grabbed her arm and pulled her from under Calvin.

"Are you okay?"

Ava was speechless. Not one word came out. She tried over and over to call Calvin's name, to yell for him to wake up, but nothing came out.

"The police are on their way!" Ava looked over at Calvin's lifeless body lying there. Her body trembled and her throat tightened with fear and sorrow.

"Don't worry. He can't hurt you anymore." Uli grabbed her robe and helped her into it. He walked her towards the bedroom door. The police entered the bedroom with weapons drawn. "Nobody move! Keep your hands in the air!"

"Officer, I am Ullrich Kärcher and this is my wife, Ava. I am the one who called you. The rapist is over there."

Uli pointed to Calvin's direction. He turned on the light.

"My wife must be in shock. She hasn't said a word since I hit this monster with my Slugger."

The police walked over to Calvin. "Call for two ambulances. This beast is still breathing. Cuff him now so we won't have to shoot him if he wakes up with trouble on his mind."

When the ambulances arrived, Ava was placed in the first one. The last thing she saw before they took her to the hospital was Calvin's body being lifted onto a stretcher. He was still handcuffed. She began to cry.

Hours later at the hospital, a female physician along with a female investigator approached Uli in the emergency waiting room.

He sat in the hard, dark blue, plastic bucket seat. His elbows rested on his widespread legs; his face buried into his opened hands. He slightly lifted his head to follow the soft voice of a female with a strong Indian accent. He slowly turned his head to the left until he saw the lips from which the voice came. A medium height woman stood there in green scrubs. Her black hair was pulled back and flowed into one single braid. Uli's eyes locked in on her beautiful face, then, he noticed a red dot in the middle of her forehead. Her name tag read "Dr. Dara."

"Your wife has been through a lot. We weren't able to find any major injuries uncommon from a rape victim. There was some slight bruising but that is to be expected given what she has gone through. We're going to let her rest for a while and hope her voice will restore itself. You can see her if you like but don't stay too long, please."

"Thank you, Dr. Dara." When he got up to go see Ava, he saw Roger entering the large hallway. Uli uncharacteristically smiled at Roger as he spoke to him, "Glad you could make it. Ava is in pretty bad shape."

"Ava? They just brought in her Opa! He had a massive heart attack on the plane two hours ago. He was trying to surprise her."

"What?!"

"What's wrong with Ava?"

"She was raped!"

"Oh my word! Where is she?"

"I was about to go in to see her. She is in a state of shock. I am just going to check in on her and then let her rest."

CHAPTER TWENTY-NINE

~~~~~~

That morning while Uli stood to pour a glass of water, he noticed Ava's eyes open quickly. With a slightly grimaced look, she said, "Oh, my back." This is the first time she spoke since the incident two nights ago.

Uli stood in shock momentarily next to her bed.

"Guten Morgen."

"Morgen, Uli."

"The police are going to ask you a lot of questions about that night. If you don't want them to, I will stay here with you and keep them away. I want you to know that your Opa is here in this hospital, too. He had a massive heart attack!"

Ava burst into tears. *It's happened again! Every time I have a crisis something happens to Opa. This could have been avoided. But, I was too selfish. Why can't I learn? When I lost my parents in the accident Opa had a mild stroke. We are connected and I know better.*

Ava tried to get out of bed but Uli stopped her. "I need to see Opa. Is he all right?"

"I don't know. I've been here with you." Ava pressed the button for the nurse. "I need to see my Opa. He's here."

"The police told me to let them know when you were alert and able to talk again."

"I will see them after I see my Opa! I am not seeing, talking or do-ing anything until I see my Opa!"

Fearing her emotions would trigger a setback for her, Uli con-vinced the nurse to allow a brief visit to Opa's room. When she got there, Roger was standing outside. For the first time in their relation-ship, Roger greeted Ava with a strong hug and kiss on both cheeks.

"Roger. How is he?"

"He is weak. And he hasn't been eating. But he is alert. He has been asking for you."

"Hereingekommen. Wie gehts es Ihnen?"

"Ich bin gut."

Ava noticed the weight loss in Opa. She noticed a slight tremble in his voice as he spoke to her.

"Opa, are you alright?"

"I am cold."

"How about I go get you a real German blanket."

"Yeah. That's what I need."

"Yes, Opa. I will go right now and bring one back for you."

"Roger, would you bring me some clothes from the house, so I can go get Opa's blanket?"

"I most certainly will, ma'am."

When she returned to her room, a police officer was there waiting. "Ma'am, I am Detective Tony Love and I am in charge of the inves-tigation concerning your case."

"Detective, I know you have a job to do but I, too, have things I must address. My Opa suffered a massive heart attack, and he's here at St. Vincent."

"Ma'am, there are some things that aren't adding up and we need answers; we need them fast. A man's freedom is depending on the answers that only you can provide. We need you to testify and keep this criminal where he belongs."

Ava closed her eyes as she replayed that night in her head. Tears welled in her eyes and she had to fight to stay standing. *Oh, my Calvin, what have I done?* She didn't know where Calvin was. She didn't know what Uli heard or if he heard anything at all.

"Detective Hug?"

"No, ma'am. It's Detective Love." He corrected her.

"Detective. I just came out of a trauma unit. You just told me your name two seconds ago and I can't remember that. My Opa wants a towel or something. I can't remember that. I have pain throbbing in certain parts of my head and my body is trembling. As a physician, myself, these factors concern me greatly and I believe hospital procedure is to provide a victim with total medical review including psychological and neurological evaluations. I don't believe I received either." She turned to Uli who had completely forgotten how well his wife knew medicine and patient's rights.

"Uli, have I received either?" She asked.

"No. No, you haven't been evaluated. You just became alert less than two hours ago," he confessed.

She turned back to the detective. "I need to be cleared by a psychiatrist before I will risk anyone's freedom," she said and sat on the edge of the bed rubbing the corner of her right temple. Detective Love backed off.

"Detective, my wife has been through quite a bit. She just found out that her grandfather suffered a heart attack. Would you allow her to do this one thing for her grandfather and then we can get her evaluated mentally so this criminal doesn't walk away on a technicality."

"Of course, Mr. Kärcher. Here's my card. I will be awaiting your call."

"Thank you, Detective."

"Thanks so much, Uli."

He nodded. "While you take care of your Opa, I have a business meeting that won't take long at all. I will catch up with you." Uli needed to give the goons new instructions and cash to get it done.

It didn't take Roger long to return from the house with Ava's things.

"Roger, we're going shopping at the Town Center. The comforter Opa is talking about is at The Pottery Barn." On the way, Ava was relieved that she had given herself some time to figure out a way to help Calvin.

"Welcome to The Pottery Barn. May I help you?"

"No thanks. We came to get one item and I know where it is." Ava kept walking in the direction of the bedding section.

"Okay. But let me know if I could be of further assistance." The clerk said as she followed a few steps behind them. Ava quickly found Opa's favorite chenille throw.

"Can you tell me where I can pay for this?"

"Oh, I can ring you up here," she said and pointed to a small kiosk to the left of them. The middle-aged woman quickly walked around to begin the checkout. She wore bangles on each arm and had perfectly manicured yellow fingernails. "Ma'am, would you like a store credit card?"

"Sure. Why not? I love this place; there's nothing like finding exactly what you're looking for, and I find it here every time. My last name is Kärcher."

"We have a Ullrich—U-l-l-r-i-c-h—Kärcher."

"Yes. That's my husband." *What did he buy here?*

"Then you are good to go. Wow, those blankets must be really comfortable. Are they?"

"Why, yes, they truly are one of the best that you carry," Ava answered and rubbed her hand across the knitted quilt. She knew Opa would appreciate the deep sterling grey and gentle woven patterns.

"You must really like those quilts because you purchased ten for your new place in Ponte Vedra. It's on the list that our interior decorator has on file. Was that service helpful and would you recommend it to anyone of your family or friends?"

"Yes, of course. They were really helpful and professional."

"Okay. Thank you, Mrs. Kärcher. Here's your temporary card, so you can do more shopping today if you like. Your permanent card will be mailed to your home in a couple of days."

"Great." Ava said but was puzzled about the new place and large purchase Uli had made. She rubbed her back to soothe the soreness. Her touch caused her to think of Calvin with sorrow. *I have to get to him.*

"Which house should we mail it to? The one in Avondale or the new house in Ponte Vedra?"

"The Ponte Vedra one and could you write the address down? I plan on doing more shopping and sending the items to that house. I don't want to drive all the way home just to get the right address. You know how it is when you buy a new house."

"I know exactly what you mean; it took me a little time to get my new address remembered at first. The older I get, the more I have to work for things that use to come easy," she said as she wrote the address on the back of Ava's receipt before handing it and the bag to her. "You have a great day and keep enjoying those blankets!"

Ava tried her best to walk calmly out of the store, but as soon as she turned through the doors and headed towards the car, she became more and more livid. Roger had never seen her stomping when she walked so he stayed close to her in case she stumbled. In his heart, she was like a daughter to him but he hadn't realized it until they hugged in the hospital. Now, she was angry and so was he. She showed him the address scribbled across the receipt.

"I don't believe this crap, Roger! Did you hear that?! Uli has a second home in Ponte Vedra? It's completely decorated by a professional decorator, my ass! There better not be a second family there!"

Ava sat in the rear of the Mercedes sedan while Roger entered the address into the GPS. Periodically she would look up as they drove the winding State Road A1A. Some of the homes were covered with vegetation. Some sat low along the road and others sat high on man-made hills. She wondered if the homes were all vacant or if life had forced families to live in such poverty. She whispered a prayer of gratitude and comfort for the homeowners. She noticed the spectacular ocean view some of the homes had for their backyard. Then, Roger abruptly stopped the car, leaned into the steering wheel and let out a gasp, "Wow!"

Ava's silence said everything: shock, disbelieve, amazement, bewilderment. She starred out the window. Both of them looked up at this majestic white house made seventy percent of glass.

"Have you ever seen such a house?" Roger asked.

"Yes. It's called a Huff Haus."

"So it's German?"

"Yes."

Ava remembered the first time she saw a Huff Haus. It was an architectural work of art. Opa and she were invited to a European builders' exhibit while they were in New York visiting Oma's gravesite. The open, pitch roof gave off the illusion that it was one with nature. She could remember Opa's pride bustling out as he went on, "This is Germany at it's best when it comes to home construction. The German reputation and durability is second to none in this body of work."

Huff Haus were the most energy-efficient houses, and the combination of glass, timber, and steel could not have been done any more elegantly.

"I can't believe this guy. Damn, Uli! After all the work I put in, all the research, and I can't begin to count the number of hours I spent briefing him. Opa would have been impressed in such a way."

This pushed Ava to the brink. Two years of research and coaching Uli. This was the German design Star Real Estate was going to reveal in the States, starting in Florida.

Let's see what you're really up to, Mr. Kärcher. Ava thought as she opened her car door to get out. The closer Ava got to the home, the angrier she became. She approached one of the workers. An elderly eastern European man with a scruffy beard stood near the house. She could tell by his dark blue overalls with straps he was from east Europe.

"Das kann dorch nicht wahr sein!" She said, extending her hand to him. He looked at her and did not respond.

"Is the lady of the house available?" He shook his head.

"Is the man of the house available?" Again. He shook his head "Five plus five is ten." Again he shook his head.

She took a closer look at the multimillion-dollar home and remembered the reason why she chose it. She loved the all-glass façade. The white shutters were a nice touch around the house bringing privacy and climate control.

Before she could ring the doorbell, she saw the most beautiful girl, a tall thin model-type. The girl saw her and bolted to the door, only to be stopped by a humongous guy. As he held her back and took her away, a short, pudgy fella came to the door.

"I'm the interior decorator from The Pottery Barn. Is the lady of the house home?"

"No! Sorry she's not."

"Are you the man of the house?"

"No!"

"Do you know when they will be home?"

"No! What have you for sale?"

"No. I'm not selling anything."

"Need we not!" He slammed the door shut.

On the way back to the car she looked in the house and noticed the gorgeous young blonde being scolded as a group of tall, lovely ladies watched.

"Okay, Roger. Take me back to the hospital so I can give this to Opa. Then I am going to find Uli! I'm going to get to the bottom of this right this minute!"

Ava smiled when she walked into Opa's hospital room. She kissed him on his forehead as she gave him the blanket. "Here you, go, Opa. How does this feel?"

"Oh, yes, this is a real blanket. Thank you so much. You are a wonderful granddaughter." Opa gestured Ava to place her ear near his lips.

"You must stay intelligent, keep your wisdom, organize your work, and stay superior. You will soon be free as the bird you are."

She smiled and nodded, then kissed his forehead again before she left. Ava had Roger drive her to Star Real Estate headquarters to confront Uli.

"Uli, can we talk for a minute?"

"Sure."

"What are you doing? Were you going to tell me about the beach house? Who and what are all those girls doing at our house?"

"I told you I had a new business plan that was going to make a lot of money. Those girls are going to be introduced to wealthy guys who can afford them a better way of life. Our company provides a service that is going to help both parties live a better life."

Ava backed away from Uli and looked at him totally confused. "Some of your clients are probably old enough to be their father or even grandfather. Those young ladies are barely legal. Those dirty old bastards aren't in this to help!" She folded her arms while the left corner of her mouth rose slightly.

Uli gently placed his hands on her shoulder and spoke softly to her, "I'm giving these girls a much better life. Some of them come from poverty-stricken homes. They are getting a way out of that and most will live much better lives than they ever dreamed."

"Introduce! I think you mean sold! Are you crazy? Who are you?"

"I am an entrepreneur! I also find people to donate organs and in exchange, I give them a piece of the American Dream. They help save a life or improve the quality of a life of someone who can afford to buy it. In return, the donator gets to live and work here in the good old U.S. of A."

"I don't know who you are anymore and what you've become, but when I talk to the police, I am going to tell them everything you just told me. Then I'm going to take them to the beach house so those girls can be returned to their families."

"First of all, I don't think you're going to do that. You see, this business is not in my name and that house isn't either. It all belongs to Star Real Estate. That's right, your precious Opa's company. You think he is having heart trouble now. Wait until his company is taken away along with everything he owns and he's rotting away in jail.

"And, Oh, and that little chocolate fix of yours, yeah, your little raven, you need to find a way to help him, too. That's right, I heard what you said before I smashed his skull. I wish I would have killed him!"

He found excitement watching the confusion swirl in her eyes.

"Look, there's Detective Love. I called him after they told me you left the beach house. I knew you would be headed back to me right away."

"Mrs. Kärcher."

"Detective Love."

"Your husband said you were ready to make a statement."

"I just want this to be over. I am alive and I am not going to press any charges."

"Well, Mrs. Kärcher, this is not an uncommon situation. The victim often doesn't want to relive it. If you don't help us with this, our chances aren't as strong."

"Detective Love, by me being the husband, what if I wanted to press charges?"

"Well, the breaking an entry we can win, but it is far less than the rape case we were hoping for."

"Detective, I may be able to help with that, too. You see I had my cell phone on record when I walked in the house."

Uli explained, "In case I didn't make it out, if anyone found it, they would know what happen."

"Let me hear it, please." The recorded evidence was not the best quality and there was a lot of movement recorded while the phone was in Uli's pocket. It also ended abruptly but Ava's pleas to stop and her begging to live were clear. Ava's encouragement at the end of the recording was not heard.

"Sir, I am going to have to confiscate your phone as evidence, and the state will pick up the case from here."

Uli gives Detective Love his phone. "Anything for justice."

When Uli played that recording, she knew Calvin would be in big trouble. Uli had her entire world in his hands: her family, the Star assets, and the man she loves.

CHAPTER THIRTY

~~~~~~

"Get me to the twenty-eight hundred block of Gainesville Street SE and fast!" Calvin's father told the taxi driver.

"Yes, sir. Is this your first time in D.C.?"

"No! We were just here, my entire family to celebrate my daughter passing the bar exam. She graduated from Georgetown University with a law degree."

"Sir, do you have an address?"

"Just keep driving. I know what her car looks like and I will know the area when we get close to her condo. I am just bad with addresses."

"Okay, sir, just tell me when."

"Thank you, Father! There's my daughter opening her car door on the right! In the red dress."

"That'll be—"

"I see how much it is. Here. Keep the change."

"Dad!"

"What are you doing here? What's wrong?"

"Your brother's in intensive care at Baptist Hospital in Jacksonville, fighting for his life!" Tears flowed from his eyes as soon as the words rolled off his tongue. He leaned over the opened car door where Cheryl stood and cried uncontrollably. He had held the hurt and fear in for eight days now. After the initial shock began to abate and her father stopped crying, Cheryl asked, "Dad, what happened?" She took his hand and walked to the back of the car to the opened trunk.

"I know things have changed nowadays but when I was coming up, you didn't as much as look at a white woman!" said Mr. Hollaway.

"Dad! What are you talking about?" Cheryl became angry.

"They have your brother handcuffed to a hospital bed and are accusing him of raping this white woman! Her husband said Calvin broke in their home and raped his wife. He crept up on Calvin and hit him in the head while it was happening!"

Cheryl took a deep breath to clear her head. "Dad," she said, "So let me get this straight. They are accusing Calvin of breaking and entering and raping this white woman in her home?"

"Yes!"

"Now I am really ticked off! If there is anything that I can be sure of, I can be sure Calvin didn't rape anyone! Those wild ass women are always throwing themselves at him." Cheryl's rage was so strong she bent the trunk of her car when she slammed it shut. "That sex was given not taken! I can't wait to get the full story from my brother!"

"I talked to your mother when I landed at the airport, she says he's in a comma."

"Don't worry, Dad. He's a fighter and he'll find his way out of this, too. Dad, did you just say you flew in?"

"Yes, I did."

"You never flew before; you always rode the train. The last time we were here you made us all ride the train. You'll do anything when it comes to your children even if they're grown."

"Yes, I will," he said. Mr. Hollaway reached in his breast pocket and pulled out two airline tickets.

"This is mine and this one is yours. We're heading back together."

"I am so proud of you, Dad."

~~~~~~

Voices singing and praying traveled the fifth floor hall of Baptist Hospital and got louder as they reached room 531. Mrs. Hollaway, her pastor, and two of Calvin's aunts were holding hands singing and praying. Cheryl joined in their tearful rendition of "I Won't Complain."

A lovely, full bloom Bird of Paradise arrangement was near his bed and another sat on the window seal. His mother said the flowers were there to bring him a little joy the moment he woke.

Uncle Bobby started a heart-wrenching prayer that was too much for Mr. Hollaway who backed out of the room.

"Mr. and Mrs. Hollaway may I speak with you both in private?" said a slender, tall, redhead doctor with sprinkles of freckles just below his eyes and a well-groomed goatee. He carried a large blue binder with Calvin's name on a sticker across the top.

"Yes." They agreed.

"I am Dr. Willie Pennick. I want to bring you up on everything we've done for your son." He said looking them directly in their eye.

"There was a lot of swelling to Mr. Hollaway's brain caused by the blow he sustained. We placed him in an induced coma to protect his brain and help prevent permanent brain damage."

Cheryl walked over to her parents and the doctor. "How long will my brother be in this coma?"

"This is our daughter, Cheryl." Mr. Hollaway said.

"That depends," he answered. "Calvin's swelling has gone down substantially in the past few days since his arrival here. So, we think it's no longer necessary to keep him in a comatose state. That is the good news."

"You say that like there is more." Cheryl said with a puzzled look.

"There could be some adverse side affects like a severe case of amnesia; if so, we have no idea how long it will last. We won't be able to tell if he will ever regain his memory. I am telling you all this because he may not recognize you at some point when you go in to see him."

Mr. Hollaway noticed his wife's breathing had become laborious. He put his arms around her and gave her a soft kiss. She rested on him for a moment and lifted her head when Cheryl spoke up.

"Thank you for explaining that for us, Dr. Pennick."

"It's no problem, Cheryl," he said.

"We really appreciate the way you are caring for my brother."

Mr. and Mrs. Hollaway's heads swung from left to right when the doctor and Cheryl spoke, as if they were watching a tennis match.

"In the state of Florida, the physician is the arbiter on when a suspect can be transferred from medical care to confinement," she said.

"Oh. Your brother can't be released. Not in the condition he is in."

The Hollaways sat in the middle of the brainstorming in amazement. Pride filled their hearts as they watched their daughter orchestrate the legal defense for her brother.

"Since there is no statue of limitations on your authority, Calvin needs as much time as he can have under your care." Cheryl emphasized the last words. Dr. Pennick nodded.

"The moment you can no longer provide that protection, our family would like to be the first to be informed before you move officially, so we can act accordingly. Could you commit to that for me?"

Dr. Pennick looked at the three pair of eyes that awaited his answer. "I'll do it." They gave a sigh of relief.

After a few days, Dr. Pennick's prediction was right. Calvin suffered with a strong case of amnesia. He had no idea who he was. He had no recollection of what happened the morning the ambulance brought him in. He had no idea why he was handcuffed to the bed.

Dr. Pennick told the family, "The brain has a way of shutting down different parts to protect itself. This might be a way of coping with what has happened. You can go in and see him but I want you to be completely aware of his situation to prevent any further damage. We will have to go slow and any acceleration to restore his memory could hurt rather than help him."

"Even if we are trying to save his life?" Mrs. Hollaway asked.

"Even if you are trying to save his life," the doctor said, nodding his head slowly. He touched Mr. Hollaway's shoulder and shook his hand. "Think about what I said. Please."

After Dr. Pennick walked away, the family's hopes of getting Calvin free were all but erased. Cheryl could see the look of despair in her parents' faces.

"Mom, Dad, I know it looks bad right now but I know we will get through this! I promise we will! I didn't go to the best law school in the nation to simply waste Calvin's money."

"Cheryl, I know you mean well and all that but a real-estate lawyer can't help us now."

"Dad, I had a double major: criminal law and real-estate law. Calvin wanted me to drop the criminal law but I wouldn't. I got a part-time job tutoring students at the college and at a high school to help pay for it. I got his back, trust me."

When they went into his room, Calvin was exactly how Dr. Pennick said he would be. It took everything they had to keep from pushing him to remember. This made Cheryl want to fight even harder. She got out of there as fast as she could. She wanted real help. She knew the doctor could keep the police away only for so long; and whenever they decided to come for him, it was not going to be gentle. She checked the Georgetown University North Florida Alumni Chapter for a list of successful criminal defense attorneys. She found Joseph Antonio Wartower, class of '69. He was still practicing at seventy years old with a success rate in the ninety-eight percentile. She called his office.

"Hello, may I speak with Mr. Wartower?"

"One second, please."

"Hello."

"Hello, Mr. Wartower. My name is Cheryl Hollaway. I got your name from the Alumni Chapter. I just earned my degree from Georgetown Law Center this pass year and passed the bar. I have a brother who put me through college and is now in trouble. I was wondering what is your fee to represent him?"

"Well, young lady, my fee is a minimum twenty thousand dollars."

"Oh, man. Let me see what my family and I can do. I thank you for your help."

"Wait a minute. You just graduated? And you passed the bar?"

"Yes, sir."

"Okay, I'll get back with you." He hung up the phone. To Cheryl's surprise, Mr. Wartower's office called back after a couple of hours and instructed her to meet him at Panera Bread in the Town Center. Cheryl agreed.

She arrived early and decided to walk around a little before the meeting. She recognized the storefront that she'd suggested to Calvin for the floral shop. The thought of him caring for his mother so much that he desired to dream big for her and acquire the new store made tears well up in Cheryl's eyes. She resisted them and began to walk toward her meeting.

When she walked through the door and looked to her right, she saw a distinguished, older gentleman wearing a long-sleeved, classic white, button up Oxford shirt. He stood up when she came near his table. His tapered hair gleamed with gray waves—much like her father's salt and pepper hair. *There's no way this guy is anywhere close to seventy. I would guess fifty tops.*

He pressed his dark blue tie against himself with his left hand as he extended his right hand to her. "Cheryl Hollaway?"

"Yes, sir. You must be Mr. Joseph Wartower?"

"Yes." The two shook hands and sat down to talk. "I did some research on you after you told me about your brother. When you said you graduated from Georgetown, I was pleasantly surprised. We didn't have that many females studying law when I was there. To find out you graduated egregia cum laude, such as I, means there is no way I can turn you down. I just have to help you out."

Cheryl started to say thank you until she noticed he had not finished.

"I believe the circumstances of your brother's case are pretty challenging, especially now that the media has told its own version. You have your work ahead of you, young lady."

Cheryl had not seen the local news and the thought of what they had reported made her weary. She took a sip of water, hoping he had more to say.

"Well, I am willing to do this pro bono. I will oversee the case but you will do most of the work. Don't worry, I will be with you every step of the way and you will get my entire team at your disposal."

"Oh, thank you so much, Mr. Wartower!" She practically yelled.

"You're part of the firm now; call me Joe. Don't worry. We are going to get your brother out of this pickle. See you at the office at five tomorrow morning."

"Yes, sir. I mean, Joe." He smiled and walked off.

CHAPTER THIRTY-ONE

~~~~~~

Ava walked down the driveway to pick up the morning newspaper. Out of nowhere, Wanda Pointer came running from across the street wearing a robe, bedroom shoes, and her hair in curlers. Wanda was Ava's high school rival. They competed for everything from Student of the Year to Homecoming Queen, since both were tall, beautiful women. Now that Wanda's weight had almost tripled, she now held the title of Miss Neighborhood Noseybody.

"Ava! Ava! Did you see all those policemen and ambulances that were out here a few weeks ago?"

"Yes, Wanda. They were at my house. It would have been hard for me to miss all that, don't you think?"

"Oh, really. That was your house?"

"Yes, Wanda. Shouldn't you be at the bakery?"

"No. It's eleven o'clock. We've been done for hours now."

"Listen, Wanda. I really have to go now."

"Oh, I am sorry. I really don't mean to keep you. It's just that I've been working quite a bit and the police have been trying to get me to come down to the station to interview me."

Wanda took her eyes from the ground and looked up directly into Ava's eyes, and with a sinister smile, she said, "I had the strangest dream that same morning when all that commotion was going on at your house. It was about two-thirtyish that morning. I was sitting in my car in the driveway. I have the same ritual every morning before I go to work. It's been the exact same thing, Ava, since we started managing Bill's crazy family bakery seven years ago. I turned on the radio to listen to N-P-R's classical music hour like always. I just love classical music, don't you? You know I use to play classical piano? I was pretty good at it, too."

Ava's throat became uncomfortably dry. She fought hard to force saliva down, so she could speak. "No. I didn't know that, Wanda. What made you stop?" Ava asked in order to keep Miss Noseybody comfortable talking. She wanted to know everything Wanda saw and everything she did that morning.

"Well, Bill and I got pregnant, then we started running the bakery, and I just put first things first, you know? Anyway, I guess I got so involved with the music I fell asleep and started dreaming. In my dream I saw this fine, Black man, and I do mean fine. What they call an Adonis! Umph! Let me tell you! From what I could see, he didn't belong on Earth. And I never look at a Black guy that way."

Wanda folded her arm and watched Ava for some reaction, any kind whatsoever would make her moment. Ava knew what Wanda was waiting for and she didn't react although her heart ached at the thought of Calvin and that night.

"Now in my lifetime I have had a few good looking men in my dreams. But like I said, it's so strange because in my day someone could get really hurt if they were remotely fantasizing or even thinking about someone of the opposite race. I know my husband would kill me! But in this dream, this Black Adonis was walking down our street. He wasn't coming to me. He was across the street at your house."

Wanda checked Ava's face once again but got the same response: nothing. She kept applying the pressure. "He stopped at that old mailbox that no one uses. He got a letter out of it and read it. He didn't just read this letter, he was studying it like he was going to be tested on it later. Afterwards he took his time and folded the letter into a little bitty square. He then forced it in that little pocket. You know the one all Levi's have just above your front right pocket. I think they call it the mini-pocket, key pocket, or something," she smacked her lips.

"After that, he walked over to the door. He didn't stop and ring the bell, he just walked right in and disappeared! Imagine that! Strange isn't it?"

Ava simply shrugged her shoulders.

"When I woke up, there were policemen and ambulances all over the place. Crazy, huh? By the way why were there so many policemen at your place that morning?" Wanda looked her directly in the eye again, awaiting for an answer. Ava just walked away without saying a word.

"Enjoy the rest of your day, Ava."

Well, Thank you Miss Nosey Body. Ava smiled and walked into the house. She called Uli.

"Yes, Ava."

"Uli, I just received a call from Detective Love. He is pressuring me to come in and make a statement. Would you please meet me at the police station? I don't want to be there alone."

"I am leaving the office right now. I'll meet you at the police station."

"Thanks. I'll wait in the car until you get here, please hurry."

"I will." When Uli showed up, he followed her into the station.

"Excuse me. We are the Kärchers and would like to speak with a

Detective Tony Love."

"Oh yes, he is expecting you. I am going to buzz you in. Please have a seat in the waiting room on your left and he will be right out," said the female desk cop.

Detective Love stood there with his hand extended. You could see his bulletproof vest through his white Oxford shirt. His hair was a fresh crew cut; his badge was clipped to his belt next to his 9mm glock. "Hello, Mr. and Mrs. Kärcher. I am so glad you could make it."

Uli and Ava shook his hand.

"Honestly and truly, Detective Love, it didn't seem like we had any other alternative by the number of times you called and the number of voice mails you left."

"We just have a zealous desire to put the bad guys in jail. Please forgive me if I gave you some discomfort, but this guy is still in the hospital and not in jail where he belongs." He gestured for the Kärchers to have a seat.

"I understand that position," Uli said.

"I am here to tell you that there is no way that I am going to revisit what happen to me that night. I am certainly not going to relive that in anyone's courtroom and certainly not in front of strangers."

"Mrs. Kärcher, I know that we are asking a lot of you to face the one who did this to you in a court of law. I must tell you that this is an open-and-shut case. The perpetrator has a severe case of amnesia, and he can't dispute anything you or your husband may say. So let's get this guy behind bars where he belongs."

Ava didn't respond. She had all but forgotten that Uli, too, could testify and have Calvin prosecuted to the fullest extent. Pain flooded her chest and she wanted to scream in agony. She clinched the muscles in her stomach and took deep breaths.

"Mrs. Kärcher, we have the cell phone recording, and we heard the attack loud and clear. The State has the right to get this criminal. I asked you to come in and provide a statement so we would not have to appeal to the courts and issue a sub—."

"Detective Love." At that moment a voice came through the intercom and interrupted the procedure.

"Yes. Do I need to remind you we are still—." He was interrupted again, "There is a Dr. Kandis Randolph who has a court order on behalf of Dr. Kärcher."

He looked at Uli, then at Ava. Uli shrugged his shoulders and shook his head slowly.

"Okay. Send her in." Detective Love relented.

A smartly dressed woman in a gray suit entered the small room. Her long thick, dreadlocks were braided into a fishtail that hung to her waist. She peeked over her glasses before she spoke.

"Dr. Kärcher has been placed under my psychiatric care." She produced her credentials along with documents issued by the courts. Detective Love looked them over and handed them back to her.

"No. Those are yours." She said waving her hand slowly. "We are of the position that you proceed without my patient's testimony. The risk of any more mental trauma is something we are not willing to take. And the medical community needs Dr. Kärcher at peek performance as quickly as possible." Detective Love looked in disbelief.

"Detective, do you really want the Mayo Clinic's lead surgeon to put herself out there in front of strangers? Do you want her to relive a rape? I can't tell you in words what that feels like."

Detective Love finally broke his silence. "The State can put me on the stand." Dr. Randolph gazed in his direction and after a few seconds she said, "You're right. You can do that. We will employ the courts to remove her name and identity from the records of this case for her immediate protection, then she'll invoke her Fifth Amendment rights. She will not go back to that night for anyone, Detective. We're done."

Dr. Randolph led Ava and Uli out of the police station. "We will not be bullied by the State."

She gave Ava her business card and shook their hands before walking away. Ava looked at the card, smiled, and thought, *First Mission: Accomplished.*

CHAPTER THIRTY-TWO

~~~~~~

Ava knew now was the time to protect Star Real Estate from the pariah. She made her next move in that direction.

"Hello. Mrs. Davis."

"Hello. Dr. Ava. How are you? The older you get the more you look like your mother."

Ava smiled. "Thanks. That means a lot coming from you. Can you pull S-R-E board minutes as filed with the state? I've gotten behind in my reading and I don't want to be lost at next month's meeting. Oh, I need the federal corporate filings, also."

"No problem, Dear." Mrs. Davis said. "I'll have them ready in a few minutes. I can fix you a cup of tea if you want to wait." Mrs. Davis knew the only person other than her boss with the knowledge, skill, and fortitude to run Star Real Estate was his granddaughter.

"No thank you, I'll just wait here," Ava said. In less than fifteen minutes, Mrs. Davis returned with the copies nicely bound in a discrete binder. She gave Ava a wink and handed her the binder and a warm, paper coffee cup with the Star logo on the side and on the lid. "Just in case you need a little taste of Germany while you review these filings. Uli brought the tea back from his second trip and no one here drinks it. Take your time reading that, dear, and keep being good to your self," Mrs. Davis made it a point to separate the "your" from "self".

Be good to YOUR self, Ava repeated to herself.

"Thanks, Mrs. Davis." Ava walked to the elevator sipping the tea. Indeed it reminded her of Oma's special blend. *Be good to your self, Ava.* Oma said softly.

"Yes, ma'am," she said looking around the office to see the spirit but Oma wasn't noticeable.

When Ava returned to the car, she enjoyed the last of the tea before spreading the papers across the back seat. She asked Roger to give her a moment of privacy. He drove slowly away from the office and found a quiet neighborhood park to wait for more instructions. Ava wasn't quite sure what she was looking for, but she believed she would know it when she saw it. After reviewing a few quarter reports and unsigned financials, Ava began to see odd patterns and red flags. Within moments, she found the smoking gun.

"Oh yeah, Uli," she whispered. "Thank you, Mrs. Davis!"

Ava called Melissa from her cell. "I am headed to your office. I have found something that could hurt my Opa and the firm."

"I'll call William over, and we will meet you in my conference room," Melissa said. Roger returned to the car while Ava ended the call.

~~~~~~

Ava shook William's hand as she walked in. After he closed the door to the small conference room hidden behind Melissa's office, the three looked at what Ava had discovered.

"Simply put my husband is into things that could ruin all of the hard work my family has done. He is involved in a corporate scheme that would destroy the firm and family and every employee."

William agreed to look into the files and locate any legal precedents.

He then suggested, "I should hold on to these documents. Melissa and I will come up with a defense. Crane will not be involved due to his loyalty to Uli. Besides, he can't be trusted and from the looks of some of this, Crane may be assisting Uli in more ways than one."

Ava did not want to part with the documents so she agreed to copy them in her home office overnight and return them in the morning.

Second Mission: Accomplished. Ava smiled and got into her car.

CHAPTER THIRTY-THREE

~~~~~~

Cheryl Hollaway walked up to the front door of Wartower and Associates at exactly 4:45am. She turned the door knob and to her surprise it opened. The first thing she noticed was a giant of a man in the corner. He was sitting in a large, comfortable reading chair with a white cowboy hat resting on his knee. His "good morning" came as a slow nod.

"Good morning," she replied. They sat in silence for five minutes when Joe Wartower emerged from his office into the main lobby.

"Four fifty! Ten minutes before five?! That's for all you civilians. Looks like you're going to pan out after all Ms. Hollaway. I really didn't expect to see you until around eight o'clock."

"My brother means more to me than you will ever understand, Joe. I would have stayed here the entire night if you told me to. My family means the world to me."

"I am glad to hear you are all in; that's going to make this a great team. Speaking of team, I would like to introduce you to Kevin Moody." Joe Wartower gestured towards the large cowboy. "He and I were in the military together. As a matter of fact, we ended up becoming best friends and marrying two sisters. Our careers for some reason have always paralleled each other's while we were in the military."

Standing at nearly seven feet tall in leather cowboy boots, jeans, and a white, long-sleeved shirt, Kevin tipped his hat and spoke, "Howdy, ma'am." His strong Southern drawl forced Cheryl to concentrate on his words. He extend his right hand to shake hers. Cher smiled, "Good morning again, Mr. Moody."

"Call me Chief or Big Country like everybody else."

"Okay, Chief"

The men let out belly deep laughs. Joe went on with his verbal resume on Chief. "See, Ole Chief headed a military police unit, and I led jag officers. So we decided to keep this police-lawyer relationship in tact. Chief is the ex-police commissioner. A lot of people still refer to him as Chief because of the legacy he left before he retired." Chief tried to downplay all the accolades by shaking his head and making strange faces. He laughed.

"Well, I like to call it semiretired. I still help the ole boys at the station from time to time with my little private investigation firm."

"That's why we work so well together because he still goes on calls and help out on some of the cases. As a matter of fact, he worked the Kärcher case that night."

Cheryl's interest peaked. To be talking with someone who was there that night excited her. "Were there any abnormalities that you can recall from that night that might be able to help my brother?"

"Well, ma'am, let me start off by saying in that neighborhood, you can really tell how rich some people are by the way they live. Those folks have money as long as train smoke. You could tell that when you walked through the door."

"What do you mean by that?"

"Every time the door opens, there was a loud, strange, cuckoo. It scared the heebie-jeebies out of me the first time I heard it," Chief shimmered and shook his head. "We found your brother's clothes neatly folded and placed in a corner right next to the bed. I never knew a rapist concerned about wrinkling clothes."

Cheryl nodded. *Yeah, that's my brother.*

"I also peeped the type of underwear that wife must having been wearing. It was still on the bed. If my wife had worn that to bed every night, we would have had more than fourteen young'uns. In addition, there was no weapon; no forced entry!"

"So, Chief, what are you saying?"

He shrugged and said, "Something in the milk ain't clean! I'll tell you what I think happened. Obviously, the husband didn't pay his butt-naked man insurance, and it lapsed."

"Huh? Chief, I don't understand a word you're saying."

"Okay, let me translate for you, Miss. In the military we have a fictional character name Jody, who takes care of the females while the men are away serving their country. While Jody, your brother in this case, and Mrs. Kärcher were practicing the horizontal mambo, Mr. Kärcher must've came home and saw that nine and half inch gift stick pleasuring his wife, and he lost it." Chief gave a small demonstration while he spoke.

"The husband grabbed the baseball bat, and he must have hit your brother in the head harder than a mule can kick! I saw the size of that hickey. Honestly, I would have done the same thing if I saw my wife taking in that much pleasure." Chief shrugged.

Cheryl listened and tried to connect Calvin with a woman she had met or someone he spoke of but she could not remember Calvin mentioning a new relationship, but her mother had. She made a mental note to get information from her mom as soon as her work was done in the office.

Chief continued. "No one covered your brother up so the boys were all talking about what they would do to their girl, if they had that type of equipment."

"So you don't think it was rape?" Cheryl asked.

"Couldn't have been. Now it's our job to prove it."

"Okay, Cheryl, you and Chief go to the station and check out what type of evidence they have. Check out everything: clothes, cell phone, vehicle, anything that can give us a clue of what really happened. I'll go talk to Calvin and let him know we are representing him. I will try to find out what he knows."

"My brother doesn't know anything. He still has amnesia and can't remember a thing from that night."

"Okay. Then I will go to the neighborhood. Someone had to see something that night."

~~~~~~

Cheryl's frustration started getting the better of her. "This does not look good," she said each word deliberately. "We've been busting our bottoms from sun up to sun down for the past three weeks, and we don't have anything."

"Don't fret something has got to fall our way," Joe said.

"I hate to sound cynical but we're going to trial in a few days, and we don't have anything substantial to help my brother." Tears filled her eyes as she spoke.

"Listen," Joe said in a firm voice, "this is where you learn what you are made of and if this criminal justice is for you, kid. You are fortunate to have experts working with you but, right now, in this very moment, you have to reach down into the core of you and determine if this is your work. If it isn't, do all your future clients a favor and stop now. But if this is the work that you were born to do, square those shoulders, stand on the legacy of our ancestors, and let's get justice for this client."

Cheryl rested her head in her open palms. Joe left her alone with his words swarming through her mind. She sat at the large conference table silently crying for nearly an hour.

CHAPTER THIRTY-FOUR

~~~~~~

Ava decided it was time to catch up with Lacey Anne, an old friend. It was Lacey who motivated Ava to further her medical career. When the two first met, Lacey was a practical nurse. Ava was a promising intern that everyone had high hopes for. In age, the two were only four months apart but in life, they were worlds apart. Lacey thought her life was cursed. She lived in the ghetto and the phrase White Trash was used to describe her daily. She had no problem cleaning bedpans and lifting patients or changing soiled linen to earn money for school. On one occasion, Ava noticed Lacey flipping through large textbooks working through medical exercises. When Lacey left behind the napkin she was writing notes on, Ava saw that Lacey had correctly answered the formula. Ava decided right then to help Lacey get into a registered nurse program, and she would support Lacey in any way.

"Ava."

"Lacey. How are you?"

"I am great."

"You look great. Ava, thanks so much for the encouragement and everything else you did to help me back then. Even those fake scholarships."

Ava put her hands on her hips. "You knew?"

"Of course! It could only have come from you. No one else with cash ever cared a damn about me."

Ava smiled. "So you're a nurse for the prison system?"

"Yes. It's has a dual role. It helps me feed my kids and see my man while he serves his remaining three years."

Ava nodded.

"I've been working out of the hospital lately, guarding patients. Boy does that bring back memories."

"Are you working with a suspect named Calvin Hollaway?"

Lacey looked surprised for a moment and answered, "Yes, as a matter of fact I am. He's quiet and folds his bedding every morning. He has this morning routine when they remove his cuffs. He immediately drops to his knees and prays." Ava could picture Calvin holding his folded clothes during their first night together. The sadness overwhelmed her but she tried to stay focused on her friend's words.

"Then, he does five hundred push ups and five hundred sit-ups before he showers. I swear it's literally five hundred!" Lacey fans herself, "It's intense to watch. Even the guards are impressed when they watch him. He's such a nice guy and gorgeous, too. He is getting a raw deal especially with losing his memory. Since he was charged, they tightened security around him but this young doctor insists that he remains under his observation until he improves. He only sees his attorney now. They say he raped some wealthy White woman." Ava watched Lacey's reaction. She shook her head slowly, "I can't believe that he would do something like that." Ava tried to keep her composure.

"I know you may have wondered why our friendship seemed to

dissolve into thin air," Lacey started confessing, "It was because of your husband, Uli. His lascivious advances were just too much for me to handle. And he's the type of man who takes 'no' as a personal challenge to push harder. I believe he sent some guy after me on the last day we talked. He was an ugly guy with this horrid scar on his face that scared me to death. I wanted to tell you but I didn't know how," Ava nodded and hugged her as she said, "I know Uli is bad news. I'm just now learning how bad he is, but I need to ask a favor if you can do it safely."

"You don't need to plea at all, Ava. I owe you so much. Whatever it is, consider it done." Ava reached in her purse and pulled out an envelope and gave it to Lacey Anne.

"I need you to give this letter to Calvin. This can help him."

"You mean—"

Ava stopped her mid-sentence. "He didn't rape me, Lacey. It was consensual. I'm in love with him." Lacey didn't respond. "I needed to tell someone who would understand and all I could think about was you and our friendship. I am in love with him and I don't want anything or anyone to harm him. If you really want to make it good with me, make sure he gets this letter. And no one else sees you."

Lacey saw the look of desperation in Ava's eyes.

"You can't tell him it's from me. Just let him know this is coming from someone who cares about him, someone who loves him. He can't let anyone know how he knows these things--neither can you."

"I understand, Ava, I really do," Lacey said.

"I am glad you do, Lacey. This helps me accomplish my mission to save everyone I love and not lose anything that matters most to me," she said.

~~~~~~

After his afternoon therapy session, Calvin returned to his hospital room to find a letter laying in the middle of his bed. He did exactly as the letter instructed and immediately requested to call his attorney. "Mr. Wartower, would you please come by? I have some info that can help with my case."

"I am on my way." After getting off the phone with Calvin, Joe Wartower gave the good news. "Ye of little faith!" He said, slamming closed his law journals and packing his briefcase quickly. "That was your brother; he sounded excited. He said he has something to help his case."

"Should I come with you?" Cheryl asked with excitement.

"I think I better do this alone."

~~~~~~

The door to the secure hospital room opened and Joe Wartower walked in with a smile as the officer closed the door behind him.

"Have you found the letter?" Calvin asked once the door closed.

"What letter?"

"A handwritten love note."

"No. There's no letter and if there was it has been destroyed."

"Check my jeans."

"My colleagues checked everything. There is no letter."

"I folded the letter really small; it's in the mini-pocket over my right leg pocket; trust me, check it again."

"Okay. I'll have them check again."

"The people who claim they are my family, I need you to get a picture of me from them. Take it with you to St. Augustine. Go to the A1A Ale Works Restaurant. Speak with the waiters named Alex and Kent. They will be able to vouch for me that the woman and I are a couple. Then talk to Catalina, the innkeeper at the Casa de Sueños

Inn. At the Casa Monica, you will need to speak with Lauren. She will remember us because we had the top suite for a weekend."

Joe Wartower jotted down the names quickly in a small notebook. "I am so glad your memory returned in time to help us with the case. The only thing I'm a little puzzled about is you referred to your family as 'those people'."

"My memory isn't back. I can't tell you how I know these things. I just know these are the places and people who can prove my innocence."

"You're giving us a lot to fight with, if this is all true," Joe said. "I will get back with you after we verify all the leads."

CHAPTER THIRTY-FIVE

~~~~~~

In his private investigator role, Chief visited each location and met with everyone Calvin named. He told the Wartower team that each lead would provide copies of receipts and reservation logs that dated back eight to twelve months. After discovering that Ava owned Schwarz, Chief even pulled surveillance video from the gym's parking lot maintenance company to see if Calvin ever met with her there.

"The good news is Calvin's leads proved to pan out. We have sound evidence and enough witnesses for our defense. But, the truth is without the love letter Calvin referred to, this was only enough evidence to prove that Calvin and Ava had a relationship not that he is innocent," Chief explained.

Cheryl listened intently. When Chief first began to explain, Cheryl felt a sense of vindication, but it quickly evolved into rage.

"My sources tell me the prosecution has evidence that will allow the detective on duty and—get this—Ava's husband to testify saying not only was it rape, but it was also brutal!"

"THAT'S A LIE!" She yelled. "SHE GAVE HERSELF TO HIM!"

"Cheryl, I know you are livid but we must be smart about this."
She nodded and held in the tears welling in her eyes. Chief reached
her his handkerchief, which she declined. "I'm mad, Chief, I am not
sad." She looked around the room to the head chair, "So what do we
do now, Joe?"

"The trial date is set. In six weeks, we will stand before state pros-
ecutors to defend Calvin's innocence—and we may also face a very
angry husband and his so-called evidence. The wife may never show
up," said Joe Wartower, "The goal is to get Calvin home now, before
that day, at any cost."

When he looked around the room, everyone nodded in agreement. Joe Wartower was proud of the team he had assembled. "So,
Chief, you tell her."

"Tell me what?"

"Cheryl, you will be operating in a more covert capacity." He said,
"The firm has set you up in a hotel and that is where you will be staying. You can't come meet with us after this evening. We will send
someone to you."

"That's not going to happen," Cheryl insisted. "What's going on?
Why do I have to stay in a hotel?"

"Chief is right. No one knows you are Calvin's sister. And now
that we have a trial date, the media is going to be all over his parents,
anyone who claims to know him, and us. You need to stay far away
from your family. Tell them not to mention anything about a sibling. You can't go visit them until after the trial. Calvin isn't going to
be asking for you. He doesn't know his parents, let alone a sibling."

Cheryl calmed down and began listening to the strategy. She
thought about it and slowly nodded. "Okay. I will make sure I take
care of that. My parents don't mind what we have to do as long as
we get him out of this mess."

Chief continued. "We know Calvin still has amnesia. So the information he provided us with came from someone, that someone had to be the person who was there with him."

"Ava!" Cheryl said with vengeance.

"Exactly. So apparently she wants to help him but in a covert way. Why? I can't tell you that. I just don't know. Since she wants to help, we are going to let her do just that. I need you to join her gym tomorrow. You have to find a way to befriend her and gain her trust." Cheryl listened closely.

"We need her help to know how to stop her husband," Joe Wartower said. "If you sense she wants to share her plight with you, tell her who you are. But only if you're sure; trust your judgment. If you are wrong, this entire thing will go up in smoke."

Cheryl nodded.

~~~~~~

Cheryl joined Schwarz during its busiest time of the day but returned the next day to workout when the gym was empty. She kept to herself in hopes of Ava coming to her. After a week of seeing Cheryl in the gym, Ava asked Sheila, "Who's the new Black girl?"

"Her name is Cheryl. She paid for a three-months membership, in cash. She does the same routine: elliptical for an hour, squats heavy every other day. The next day she does the treadmill and upper body. She doesn't talk with anyone. But God she has a beautiful smile and high cheekbones. Seems friendly, too."

"Sometimes you just have to be the one to break the ice. I'll show you how it's done." Ava smiled and walked over to Cheryl.

"Hi, I'm Ava. If you ever want to try something different you could come to our spin class one day." It took everything in Cheryl's soul to remain calm and be cordial.

"Hi, I am Cheryl. No, thank you. I don't know if I could concentrate in a class. I have too much on my mind."

"I know what you mean. I have had a lot on my mind lately. And you're right, it is a little difficult," Ava said.

"I'm new here. I don't know anyone. I'd love to talk but I just don't want to burden people," Cheryl said. Then she noticed the Leo Jordan insignia on Ava's uniform. *My God. Leo!*

"It wouldn't be a burden if you wanted to share with me." Ava's voice interrupted Cheryl's thoughts.

"No. I mean. Well, I don't want to give you the wrong idea. I am just thinking about a family member heading to jail. He's not a criminal; he just was in the wrong place at the wrong time and apparently he was doing the wrong thing."

Ava froze and gazed off into space. Cheryl cheeks and her eyes were so familiar. *I know this face.* Ava thought.

Cheryl rushed, grabbed her towel, and said, "Thanks for listening I have to go." A tear raced down her right cheek as she turned and entered the locker room. Ava also had tears racing down her cheeks as she followed Cheryl into the locker room.

"Listen, I have a friend locked up for something he didn't do either. I love this man more than I have ever loved any man and I will do anything to get him out."

Then you need to do something about it! I should whip this bitch's ass.

Joe Wartower's voice registered in Cheryl's head and a cooler spirit took over.

"I love my guy too, more than I can tell you."

"Sounds like we are kindred sprits," Ava said as another tear fell.

"My brother, Calvin, doesn't deserve to be locked up."

"Calvin Hollaway?"

"Yes. He's my brother."

A river of tears began to fall from Ava's eyes. Her body shook.

210

She was breaking down. The weight of this trouble was more than she thought she could bear. She needed this moment. Cheryl waited until Ava collected herself. Between her whimpers, she said "Cheryl, we can't talk here. Meet me somewhere." She took a deep breath. "Meet me at the Clara White Mission on West Ashley. I know the current C.E.O. We can talk in the conference room without worrying about anyone seeing us."

Ava chose to meet at The Clara White Mission for a few reasons. She remembered the long-standing relationship her family had with the mission. Oma always said if you ever need a place to run to for safety, the Mission was where to go.

Oma often talked about the day in 1939. It was the day they met Roger as a little boy. He couldn't have been no more than six years old. Opa and Oma had just arrived on the streets of downtown Jacksonville. They were tired and hungry when Roger walked them a few blocks to Ashley Street. There stood a long line of Negroes waiting for food. Opa thought they wouldn't feed his family but when they reached the front Miss White smiled and fed them, too. The moment the family's income stabilized, Opa decided that Miss White's organization would be the only charity he would support in money and in time.

"What time?" Cheryl asked, trying to stay composed.

"I can be there at three," Ava said.

"Okay."

~~~~~~

Ava stood in front of the building as Cheryl arrived.

"I see you're early," Cheryl said with a smirk.

"Yeah, your brother has rubbed off on me in more ways than one."

The women walked through the center and greeted everyone they passed until they entered the corner conference room.

"So, Ava, you really love my brother."

"Oh my God, Yes."

"Okay." Cheryl picked up her cell phone and said, "Okay, Chief. You can come in." When he did, Cheryl introduced them.

"Pleasure to meet you, ma'am."

"Likewise, Chief Moody."

"Please, call me Chief or Big Country like everyone else does."

"Okay, Chief."

"Now, tell me, how did we get in this pickle?"

"I made some stupid mistakes," Ava confessed. "And now I need to fix this before it gets any further. First of all, I never told Calvin I was married. So he's not an adulterer. Second, I thought my husband was going to be in Europe longer. Late that night, I had a desire for Calvin, so I invited him into my home for the first time. I know. Another stupid mistake! Uli returned two days earlier and caught us role playing."

J.C. Pitnam knocked gently on the door. "This looks like you are going to be here a while, so I brought you some coffee."

"Oh, that's good," Chief said. They remained quiet while J.C., who was the new owner of the Mission, offered each of them cream and honey. She slipped out the room as quietly as she had entered. After a few more sips, Chief placed his empty mug on the table and asked Ava to continue.

"Well, the next thing I knew, I heard a loud pop and Calvin's body collapsed on top of me. Uli had hit him in the head with something and almost killed him!" Ava began crying and shaking. "This is entirely my fault, Chief! I did this! I gave myself to him! He didn't take me! Help me make this right. This was not rape!" She cried.

"Why haven't you told the detective this story?" Chief asked. "Uli has framed my family, all our board members, our executives. He has also wrapped the company assets in illegal, fraudulent activities. He has made all of it point to Opa who knows nothing about it! My Opa is much too old to sit in jail!" She cried more.

"So it's okay for my brother to go to jail? You spoiled bitch!" Cheryl got up and rushed toward Ava.

"Nooo!" Ava screamed in defense.

Chief caught Cheryl.

"Whoa. Whoa. Whoa. Calm down everybody." Joe Wartower said as he entered the conference room.

"I'm so sorry, Cheryl. I didn't mean it that way. I'm going to help get Calvin out!"

"I know you will!" Cheryl said pointing at her. Chief walked her back to her seat and asked her to calm down.

"Okay, Ava, I have arrested a lot of criminals in my day. What type of illegal activity is your husband involved in?"

"Human trafficking and organ theft, for starters," she said quickly. "He's smuggling people—young girls, teenagers, all pretty and even a few young boys and men into the country just to take their organs. After he gets their organs, he sells them on the Black Market. He then forces the donors to work off some make-believe debt they will never be able to pay off. I don't want to even imagine what he does with the girls! I don't know who this monster is!"

The entire room stayed quiet as they all processed the gamut of this guy's dealing right under their noses. "Well, young lady, I know he seems different to you. But to me it's a familiar scene. He's a criminal. They all share one thing in common: every last one of them thinks they have the recipe for the perfect crime. But to be honest with you, they yearn to brag about it. For it to be valid to them, someone has to know they got away with it. And when he confesses, we'll be there to report it and put him where he belongs—right behind bars.

So let's start thinking of a plan," Chief said and leaned on the table.

For nearly three hours, the Wartower team argued strategies, legal restrictions to entrapment, state precedents, and criminal charges. They surveyed each other's strengths and their roles in the new plan. It boiled down to Ava and Cheryl teaming up.

"Here's where you two ladies are going to come in. Cheryl, with your real estate knowledge and degree, you're going to intern at Star Real Estate. Ava, we are going to need four intern positions opened as soon as possible so this will look legitimate. Can you make that happen?"

"Yes I will talk to H.R., and the internship will open this week."

"Cheryl, you have to find a way to grabs Uli's attention."

"That won't be hard," Ava said with a laugh, "I know my husband, Uli, and as for getting his attention, just look at Cheryl. She has everything that he craves: she's beautiful, she's tall, she has a body to die for, and she's young."

"Good. So you ladies decide on the start date, what to bring, and how things work over at Star Real Estate. Then, let's get this creep before he gets Calvin."

CHAPTER THIRTY-SIX

~~~~~~

Uli walked into his office and approached his secretary. "Ms. Ruth. I've noticed we have an African-American female intern that's been here for the past couple weeks. That's a first for the company, isn't it?"

"Yes, sir," replied Ms. Ruth. "She has a law degree with concentration on real estate law. She graduated top of her class and has already passed the bar. The board decided if we are to stay competitive, we needed to be more diverse."

"She seems to be pretty dedicated; the other interns leave at quitting time but she stays late. I've even noticed her at the bus stop a few times when I was leaving. I think we should let her see how things work at the executive level. I would love to mentor her."

"I think that's a good idea, Mr. Kärcher."

Uli walked out of his office and approached the girl.

"Miss, may I speak with you for a second?"

"Yes, sir. Did I do something wrong?" Cheryl asked.

"No. On the contrary, my name is Uli Kärcher." He did his pitch. Letting her know he was the Vice President at Star Real Estate. Telling her about the company's commitment to diversity. He even let her know he noticed her dedication and believed that her talents were being wasted at the current level. "I am willing to offer myself as your mentor at the executive level. Would you be interested?"

"Yes, sir."

"What's your name?"

"Cheryl, Mr. Kärcher."

"I know a man isn't suppose to ask a woman her age but do you mind if I ask?"

Cheryl smiled. *Ava knows her man.*

"No. I don't mind at all. I'm twenty-three."

Uli thought, *Young, chocolate, thin, ambitious. Nice combinations.*

Cheryl assisted Uli for two weeks, turning down his request every evening to give her a ride home rather than take the bus.

This evening a severe thunderstorm started as Uli drove out of the parking garage. He stopped at the bus stop. "Get in, Cheryl, I am not taking 'no' for an answer, not in this weather." Cheryl took his offer and got into the car. Uli gave her his handkerchief. She wiped her face and noticed him staring at her blouse which stuck to her breast.

"Where do you live?" Cheryl gave him the address and when he pulled up to the hotel he asked, "You live here? In a hotel?"

"Yes."

Uli saw an opportunity to make a play, and he didn't hesitate. "Okay, listen. I know it can be hard for an intern. You can earn some extra money if you are okay with waitressing a party. I am inviting some wealthy clients to participate in a new venture. I will also be celebrating a legal victory that same evening." He said in a boastful tone.

"I'll let you know the particulars when I have the exact date. Would you be interested?"

Inside Cheryl was ecstatic as she thought, *This. Just. Might. Work!* "Sure. I can always use some extra money. I hate being in this place. That's another reason why I stay late at the office."

"Great, we can help each other out." Uli leaned over and quickly kissed her on the cheek and rubbed her thigh as she exited the car.

This Uli guy is nothing but a dirty old man.

Cheryl called Ava to setup a meeting with Chief. *It's taken nearly five months and things are finally bringing us closer to my brother's freedom.*

CHAPTER THIRTY-SEVEN

~~~~~~

A petite woman with deep dark eyebrows and wavy hair just as dark as her eyebrows walked into Joe Wartower's office, her skin only half a shade lighter than a Kenyan. She approached the secretary and said, "He no rape." Mr. Wartower's secretary looked and said, "What?"

"He no rape her."

"Who?"

"Man on T.V. He no rape her. Your Joe War man is to help him."

The secretary got up to get Chief who was relaxing in the other office, on the couch like a beach whale. "Chief, I can't understand a thing this woman is saying. You got to come out here and see what she is trying to tell me." He walked out and she immediately started again. "He no rape her."

"Who didn't rape her?"

"The man on T.V."

"You know him?"

"No. Senor."

"So how do you know he didn't rape her?"

"My father is Ebanjulist. He say always tell truth."

"Her father is what?" The secretary asked.

"She said he's an Evangelist."

"I no have house so I sleep in car. Two car come. Senor get out. Senorita get out. They dance. I tella you. She in love. Give her heart. Give her all."

"Thank you. What's your name?"

"Manuela."

"We may need you to tell this to more people, will you?"

"Always tell the truth. My father Ebanjulist. I in my car at fireworks store with my baby."

Chief smiled and shook her hand.

~~~~~~

Uli met with his personal lawyer to check on the status of the case against Calvin Hollaway. He hated the sound of that name.

"Uli. How are you?" Attorney Michael Wayne Moore said.

"Fine. How are things going with the trial?"

"They are fine. Well, we might have a small snag."

"What do you mean?" Uli asked with a concerned look.

"Do you think your wife knew this guy? He might have been a good friend."

"Are you accusing my wife of cheating?" Uli confronted the young attorney.

"No! It's just that a witness said she saw them dancing in the Phantom Fireworks parking lot off 95 South. She sleeps there at night, and she is willing to testify to what she saw."

"No, she's wrong. I'll have someone check it out. That won't be a problem. I promise you that." Uli said and quickly walked out the door.

That night Uli pulled into Phantom Fireworks parking lot. He saw an old, beat up station wagon parked. He walked over to it and saw Manuela and her little girl playing.

"Hello, Senor."

"Hello. Is that your little girl?"

"Si."

"How old?" Uli asked as he rubbed the black gloves he was wearing on his hands together.

"Dos." Manuela began to sense evil so she pressed the automatic locked button. A look of rage from Uli soon followed.

Just then, a St. Johns County sheriff pulled in the parking lot. He got out his patrol unit. Noticing the classical music blaring from the dark Mercedes, he slowly surveyed the car and took mental note of the license plate. He watched Uli's behavior when he greeted him, "Hello, sir." He stood between him and Manuela's door. "Manuela, have you and Pariss eaten tonight?"

"No." She said and kept her fearful eyes on Uli.

"That music is kinda loud for the people of St. Johns County," he said looking squarely in Uli's eyes. Uli took three steps backwards then turned towards his car. The sheriff watched Uli until he could no longer see the backlights.

He peeked in the car and smiled at Pariss. Manuela unlocked the door. The officer unbuckled the carseat and pulled the baby and the seat out. Manuela got her things—which were only a few but they were clean. "Lock your doors. I will have someone come get this car; it's seen it's last days. You are coming back home with me." T two drove off in the patrol car as Uli watched from the top of the Interstate.

CHAPTER THIRTY-EIGHT

~~~~~~

When Ava walked in the meeting, Chief told her, "There's something different about you, Mrs. Kärcher. You are glowing." Ava rushed over to the nearest trash can and heaved. Since meeting Cheryl and starting to work for Calvin's freedom, she hasn't been able to hold any food in her stomach, only tea and smoothies.

"Yep. That's it, you're pregnant," he said with a smile.

"No, I am not. Uli and I are not physical. We are just room-mates."

"Young lady, there are two things that I know I do well, being a father and being a police officer. I know what I am looking at, trust me. Do you honestly think my wife went through this fourteen times and I didn't learn anything?"

Cheryl walked in the room talking fast, "Okay, Chief, listen. Uli asked me to work a party he is planning for some high-end clients and to celebrate winning the trial."

"Did he tell you when?" Chief asked.

"No. He said he would let me know."

Joe Wartower said, "Okay that means it's about to go down and soon. Remember I told you that all criminals have to let someone know they are responsible for a crime and this guy won't be any different."

"Mrs. Kärcher, Do you mind wearing a wire? I feel if there is anyone he would want to brag to, it would be to you."

"No, I don't mind. I just want Calvin out of this mess."

"Cheryl, we will need you to wear a wire also so you can be our ears and eyes inside the party. We are hoping the party will be at the Ponte Vedra location. While inside you will let us know where everyone is positioned so when we storm the place, there will be few incidents. There is a vacant house directly across the street. The St. John's sheriff's officers and I will be positioned there. So if anything goes off plan, we will rush the place. Is everyone okay with their assignment?"

Both ladies agreed.

CHAPTER THIRTY-NINE

~~~~~~

Uli made a call to the district attorney. "Hello. I am Uli Kärcher and I would like to know what is preventing my case from going to trial? How long are you going to allow this rapist to run freely?"

"Mr. Kärcher, we are in contact with your attorney. He should keep you abreast on what is on the schedule and what the delays are." Uli begged his pardon and hung up.

Uli asked his secretary to have Cheryl come to his office. "Hello, Cheryl, do you remember me asking you a while ago about waitressing a party for me?"

"Yes, I do."

"Well, I am thinking we have enough waitresses by the last count. Would you be interested in being a hostess?"

"Yes. That is fine with me."

"Okay. It's tomorrow in Ponte Vedra. Here is the address. I will send a car for you. Oh, yes. I almost forgot. Here is your stipend for an evening dress. There is also enough for a hair salon."

"Man. The company sure knows how to treat a woman."

Uli smiled. "We try our best. You need to be there by 3 p.m. to

223

make sure you meet up with my two colleagues. They will instruct you from there on what to do. I won't be there until about 8 p.m. I will go to the airport to meet and greet our clients, and we will then caravan to the location."

"Okay, Mr. Kärcher. See you tomorrow."

Cheryl met Chief and Ava at the Mission.

"Okay. Uli told me it's going down tomorrow. They are flying everyone in and it's all a go."

"Okay. Mrs. Kärcher, rather than go to the gym in the morning, you need to come here. Use the rear entrance so no one will see you come in. We will be waiting to wire you up."

~~~~~~

The morning of the trial, Ava showed up at the mission before the crack of dawn.

"Chief, I hope you are right about this."

"Trust a good ole country boy. If I tell you a hen dips snuff look under her left wing."

Chief and his assistant took extra care to wire Ava discretely and covering the microphone with her clothing. She hugged him, "Thank you, Chief, wish me luck." Ava returned home.

Uli sat at the breakfast table when she came in.

"How was your workout?"

"It was fine."

"So how do you think your little raven feels knowing this is the last time he is going to be out of his cage for a while?"

"Uli, why are you doing this? You have won. I am doing everything you want me to do. I am with you and you still feel you need to send Calvin to jail."

"You did this! When you brought him into our home, you decided he needed to be destroyed!" Uli said as he slammed his fist on the kitchen table.

"This is not your home. This is my home! My family home! You came here and brought your stuff here," Ava yelled at Uli for the first time in their marriage. Looking him directly in his dilated pupils that were the size of two pregnant fleas. He yelled, "Now it all comes out! Your true feelings finally come out!"

"I am the one who has done everything from the very beginning. But all I got from you was a pity party! 'I should be this.' 'I should be that.' Not once did you put us first. You didn't know I knew you were screwing over me!" Ava fought back.

"I brought that company out of the ashes! I made it profitable! The life you all enjoy is over my back, you and that crusty old man! So if I screwed over you with anyone, it was because I deserve it!"

"That's exactly what I thought! And if I'm going to get screwed I might as well get screwed by something big enough for me to enjoy!"

"You bitch!" Uli snatched the blouse right off of her and all the wires were exposed. "You didn't think I knew you were wired? You must think I am some type of idiot. I had you followed this morning, and it's a good thing I did."

Uli was the color of a ripe tomato.

"Why would you be going to a mission this early in the morning? I was born at night, but it wasn't last night! You're still trying to save that raven, you silly woman! What did you think I would say for your stupid wire? That they should drop the case and let him go free? That I forgive you and him? That he's innocent? I would never!" Ava kneeled down on the floor in tears. He raised his hand to hit her.

Roger burst into the room. "Ava! Ava! It's your Opa! He's having another heart attack! Call for an ambulance!"

Grabbing her blouse, Ava rushed to the nearest house phone downstairs. Uli rushed up to Opa's side. He saw Opa lying in the bed grasping for air, fighting to stay alive.

"You old idiot! I gave you everything I had and you gave me your ass to kiss. Well, it's okay. It's a pity your family is going to lose everything for something you had nothing to do with. It serves you and that idiot granddaughter of yours right. Did you know she crossed the color line with a Black man? Adultery with a Black guy, who does that? Well, I guess that's how you raised her. You can thank her from the prison cell you will rot in. The trafficking that's going to take place tonight, is all going on in a house that I bought. Yes. I bought the house, but of course it was purchased with funds from your company, using your signature! How does it feel to know you will be the one paying for all those illegal workers with prison time! I want you to know every Town Center that the company built was built by illegal workers, each and every one of them, and I orchestrated it all and made it point to you. You will rot in jail, ole man! All the money laundering, points to you. Illegal organ sales point to you. This master plan only had one failure, that is I won't get to see you waddle in it because I am flying out of here tonight!"

"No, I am afraid you won't be going any where. We got all of your confession on tape." Detective Love said as he walked dangling handcuffs. Opa smiled as he exposed his wires and pointed at them.

"Ullrich Kärcher, you have the right to remain silent. Anything you say can and will be used against you," were the last words Opa heard as the detective walked Uli out the door.

"Chief, why didn't you tell me about using Opa?"

Before he could answer, Opa said, "Because he didn't know. It wasn't his idea. It was Cheryl's plan. With all the times you met at the mission, did you really think that J.C would leave me out in the cold? I knew every move, every step of the way."

"Well, I have my own secret to tell you all," Ava confessed.

"Oh, yeah? What is it?" Chief asked, knowingly.

"You were right, Chief. I am pregnant and it's with Calvin's baby." She turned to look at her grandfather, "Opa, Are you okay with that?"

"Ava, do you love him?"

"Oh, yes! Opa, I do."

"All children who come out of love are always good. And our blood line continues on."

~~~~~~

Cheryl stood behind the massive table reserved for defense attorneys and presented the court and the district attorney with all the evidence from Wartower and Associates. Calvin proudly watched her. *Confident, poised, articulate. All Hollaway. Way to go, Sis.*

"Due to new evidence presented by the defense in the case of the Great States of Florida vs. Calvin Hollaway, all charges have been dismissed. Mr. Hollaway, you are free to go."

As soon as the judge struck the gavel, Calvin's family rushed to congratulate him. Calvin extended his hand to shake his father's. He pulled him close and whispered in his ear, "If you are on time, you're late."

"You remember!" His father yelled.

"Yes. My memory started coming back two days ago. I couldn't tell anyone because no one came to visit me." Everyone laughed.

The entire family celebrated, hugging, shaking hands and a few tears were dropped.

Everyone stopped as Ava, Opa, and Gertrude approached.

Ava ran into Calvin's arms. She cried and kissed him.

"I think Ava wants to talk with you." Opa said.

"You all know, Ava?" Calvin asked, holding her side.

"Yes." Everyone answered.

"Calvin. This is my Opa, Helmet Lang."

"Pleasure to meet you, son."

"The pleasure is all mine, sir." Calvin said shaking Opa's extended hand.

"Go on, Ava, tell them." Opa said proudly. Ava hesitated and then said. "I am so afraid to say it," she said, looking first at Cheryl then Calvin.

"Say it, baby," Mrs. Hollaway said.

"Yes, say it," Cheryl said, "We've already been through alot together."

"Well," Ava started, "Both of our families are getting small limbs."

"Huh?" The Hollaways said.

"I'm pregnant with Calvin's baby."

The cheers in the courtroom could be heard for miles.

CPSIA information can be obtained at www.ICGtesting.com
Printed in the USA
LVOW07s0043170516

488516LV00002B/3/P